Cherry Pie

A TABOO WHY CHOOSE NOVELLA

DAISY'S DELIGHTS
BOOK ONE

DAISY JANE

Copyright © 2022 by Daisy Jane

All rights reserved.

No part of this book may be reproduced in any form or by any electronic or mechanical means, including information storage and retrieval systems, without written permission from the author, except for the use of brief quotations in a book review.

The story, all names, characters, and incidents portrayed in this production are fictitious. No identification with actual persons (living or deceased), places, buildings, and products is intended or should be inferred.Proofreading done by Geeky Girl Author Services, LLC.

Cover design | Daisy Jane

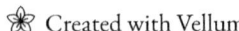 Created with Vellum

Welcome to Daisy's Delights

Welcome to Daisy's Delights!
   On the menu:

Over the top, extreme, and completely ridiculous erotica shorts meant to fix a craving.

Everything's why choose, but I have a variety of flavors for every palette.

In this selection, you're getting a step dad and step brother's, age gap, why choose romance with a heavy dose of breeding and a side of lactation.

If you're looking for a steak, you won't find it here. I'm only serving sweet 'n' naughty treats.

Got a sensitive tummy? Check the content labeling before you indulge.

Now go on and enjoy. You deserve it.

Nutrition Facts

∞ servings per container
Serving size   3.4 ml or 3/4 tsp

Amount per serving
Calories   0.7

	% Daily Value*
Total Orgasms	100 %
Group Orgasms	75 %
Dad's Watching 'Gasms	25
Eiffel Towers 50mg	45 %
Milk 25mg	78 %
Unhinged Mason Men 200g	100 %
All Fours 100g	100 %
Put A Baby In Her 69g	
	%†
Protein 5,000g	
Reality	0%
Plot	0%
Reason	0%
Seriousness	0%

* The % Daily Value (DV) tells you how much smut in a serving of Daisy's Delights contributes to a daily smut diet. 2,000 pages a day is used for general sleezy advice.

† One serving adds 69g of happiness to your day and represents 69% of the Daily Value for smut consumption.

INGREDIENTS:
FRUIT (CHERRY), CREAM PIE, DADDY COMPLEX, DVP (MAY ALSO CONTAIN TVP), EIFFEL TOWERS, LUBE (SPIT, WATER-BASED, OTHER), HOT LAWYERS, SKIMPY DRESSES, BRATTINESS, THREE GROWN MEN, AGE GAP, STEP DADDY, STEP BROTHERS, "LEAVE SOME FOR YOU DAD, BOYS", BREEDING (MAY CONTAIN PREGNANCIES), REVENGE, "YOU LOVED ME ALL ALONG?", TEASING, WORKPLACE SEX, BATHTUB ORGASMS, SHARING, LACTATION.

MAY CONTAIN RIDICULOUSNESS.
MANUFACTURED BY DAISY'S DELIGHTS

One

"I'm not ready for you to go," I admit sheepishly, both proud of myself for saying the words yet equally feeling foreign being so vulnerable. I'm not one to spew feelings all over, especially directing them towards the person they're *actually* meant for.

But Marianne is different.

She strokes a weathered hand down my hair, taking a moment to fish her fingers through the ends soothingly like she did when I was a child after picking me up from school.

"I know, *mon cherie amér.*"

Sinking into a high back barstool at the kitchen island, my chin sinks into my curled knuckles, elbows keeping me off the cool granite. I let out a deep, heavy sigh, one that contains the misery of more than this day, but I'm using this moment to relieve my heart and mind of *a lot* of different pain.

"You are grown now. You don't need me like you once used to," she says in her heavy French accent. Her smile trembles a bit, as if the truth of those words hurt her more than actually having to go.

"I do need you," I argue, because *she* is the only one I have. As if she doesn't know it, I remind her. "You're all I have, Mari." The words are soft and crumbly, like one of her fresh baked chocolate and cherry cookies. I'll miss those cookies, but that isn't even in the top ten things I'll miss about Mari.

She tips her head to the side, her expression tenderly defiant. "That *isn't* true."

"It is," I argue back. Though I'm feeling *all* the pain of her looming void, fighting is how I protect my feelings and distract myself from *how* I feel.

After one more sad and unsatisfied smile—*Mari is the only one to cut through my bullshit without a single word*—she turns to the sub-zero refrigerator behind her. The doors shine; they sparkle really.

I live in a home where surfaces sparkle and gleam, where disinfectant and home-cooked meals fill the air at all times. A place where sheets have the corners tucked under the mattress, like a hotel.

My home is large.

In fact, it's more of an estate than a home—as it employs several people at all times. The floors gleam, everything has a place and rests in its place, there are no shoes strewn about, no empty package boxes on the floor, nothing left to sit idle and collect dust.

The entire place is a well-oiled and beautiful machine.

Yet I have the selfish audacity—*I've been told*—to hate my life. To hate this house.

And the people that live here. The same people Mari is referring to.

She pours the tea she retrieved from the sub-zero into a glass and pushes it my way. "Cold tea will help your spicy mood."

I take a sip of the tea, but it only serves to make me more bitter. Mari makes the most delicious sun tea and this drink only reminds me that I won't have it again after today. Not like this, at least. But I drink it because I love her, and as much of a brat as I can be, I won't be hurtful on her last day.

I'll still fight a little, of course, because I can't have her leaving here thinking I'm suffering from some medical stroke or something. But like usual, I'll keep the big rifts for *them*. Not her.

"Are your kids excited to see you?" I ask *foolishly* because *of course* her kids want to see her, grown or not. She nods. "Other people waiting to welcome you back?" I ask but I know the answer.

Of course, she does. Because everyone has someone, right? Even though Mari has been living in this home raising me for the last fourteen years, I also know she's in her late sixties and has a network of people she loves back in France.

"*Everyone*," she says with a smile so broad that I feel jealous and guilty all at once.

"You should have left sooner," I quip, sour and bitter, hating to dish her up this side of myself on her last day but honestly sometimes, I'm so angry at *them* that I can't control whether or not I dish it out to others. My emotions have always been hard for me to understand and wrangle.

"Ah, *ma fille amère*, do not get testy with me today." After returning the pitcher of tea to the refrigerator, Mari joins me, taking the seat next to mine. Her peppered hair looks a lot whiter as the sun drops across it from the window. Her hands are worn from taking care of me for so many years. She pats my thigh. "You will be okay, but Cherry, you must *let* yourself be okay. Do you know what I'm saying?" she asks, her French accent making every single statement sound so smart and sharp.

I drink the tea and look forward, unwilling to tell her that I know *just* what she means. Be kinder to them, she means, and I know this because she's said as much many times before.

How can I be kind to them? How can I open myself to them when *one* of them couldn't even be bothered to take a hand in raising me? Despite the fact that it was his *legal* obligation, he hired Mari to raise me under his roof. Now with her leaving, I'm left with complete strangers; I am *living here* with complete strangers.

"Will you write?" I ask, bypassing her questions. She's used to me, so she sighs and moves on.

"I can write paper and envelopes. No email for me. I plan to go home and dewire."

"*Unplug*," I correct because even after over a decade in America, Mari's English is still a bit... *confused*. Staying inside an estate all day, every day, will do that to you, though.

"Yes, unplug," she says while placing her cell phone on the island, screen facing up. "I won't miss this." She spins the phone on the surface.

I stare into the amber liquid as my fingertips chase beads of condensation down the wall of my glass. "I'll miss you so much, Mari," I say quietly like it's a secret. It isn't, though, but I am trained to keep my voice down when admitting things that are important. To keep my deepest feelings separate from this house and its residents.

"It is goodbye but not forever. When you are ready, you can come to France and visit me."

I finish the tea, and no more than ten minutes later, an Uber awaits in the long, gravel driveway in front of the house.

"They didn't even come to see you off," I say more to

myself than to her, though it is directed at her. "Fucking pricks."

"*Ma fille amère*," she soothes, and the gentleness of her tone sends pops of heat behind my eyes. I blink, refusing to acknowledge them because I don't cry and am not weak. "You must soften yourself for this world, Cherry. How can love ever find you if you are too hardened to be moved?"

She wraps her body around mine in a long, meaningful hug. This is the last time I'll feel her heart beating against my chest as she holds me. I can't fight the tears that fall, but I still choose to ignore them.

"Take care of yourself but don't forget, there is a middle between every two loose ends."

I roll my eyes and she laughs at me, and the wind brings leaves to our feet as the sun puts warmth at our back. The gravel crunches as her measly two suitcases are loaded into the trunk, courtesy of the driver.

"I love you. And being in France won't stop me from loving you." She takes my chin in her soft hand and my face fills with fire so painful and searing that I close my eyes in an effort to escape it. But when they open again and are met with her damp cheeks and partial smile, I know I can't hide.

"I love you, Mari," I whisper, having never said those three words to anyone else in years. And when I say them, I know there's a very good chance I won't say them again to anyone, ever.

"Promise you will visit. If you ever want to, he will pay for you to come."

I tuck my long hair behind my ear as the wind gathers at my back, tossing the ends over my shoulder. "I'm welcome to visit and yet I am not allowed to come live with you."

Another sideways head tip paired with a tilt of her lips. "He doesn't want you to come with me."

I know it's true. I know it is. Because the fight we had the night I begged to go to France with Mari is etched into my brain as well as my own name.

"I don't care what he wants," I say, sounding and feeling childish, but I can't help it. He brings the immature, angry, fiery, vein-popping side out of me like no one else. I should just stomp my foot, my words would sing-song nicely to the beat of a temper tantrum.

"But *I do*. Because he was a loyal employer to me for years, my darling. You don't have to believe or like it, but he was good to me so *I* am good to *him*." She hugs me again, and presses kisses to each of my cheeks. "I was contracted until you were eighteen. The contract is fulfilled. Now I must go."

I nod. And we just stare at one another for a bit. Moments, minutes, I don't know. All I do know is that I can't get enough of her rich, dark eyes and her graying hair, the smell of *Shalimar* on her wrists or the soft swish of her linen pants. Everything Mari will be missed.

I want to say *you have been a mother to me. You have been my only mother, because my own mother went and got herself killed when I was just five so I hardly remember her at all. If any.*

Mari has been my mother. She has been here since the first week after mom was murdered.

She has taught me everything. When I say everything, I don't mean *some* things. Not only do I say what I mean but she really has shown me the ways of life.

Cutting hair, baking, cleaning, riding a bike, getting out of class with "woman" trouble, how to use a tampon, painting my nails, styling my clothes, reading, writing, literally everything.

The door slamming closed jars me from my painful tumble down memory lane. My eyes meet hers across the lowered car window. The sweaty man in the driver's seat drums his thumbs along the wheel as he waits for us to say goodbye.

"Goodbye, Cherry." Mari's eyes are misty again and I refuse to acknowledge that mine aren't much better. "Be good to them. They are not bad. *Sometimes things aren't what they seem.*"

"Bye, Mari." Those are the only two words I can manage. Tiny bits of granite and river rock pop from under the tires like jumping beans as the car exits the long driveway.

Be good to them, she says. I shake my head as I make my way back inside the empty home.

Why should I be good to them when they are no good to me?

Up the stairs, I make my way into my bedroom where I close and lock the door and bury my head into a pillow. The only thing I trust with my sobs.

And I cry in private until I hear the cars outside and know *they* are home.

My stepfather and his two sons.

Two

Can you make it feel like home if I tell you you're mine? The lyrics float above me as I stare up at all the green glowing stars on the ceiling. Lana Del Rey is where I turn when I'm really lost because knowing someone else is miserable too is relieving in some sick way.

There's a solid knock at my bedroom door.

I have my own floor, and they give me a wide berth. That leaves just one person it could be now that Mari is back in France.

"Sylvio?" I call out the name of the man who runs this house. I don't know what title he has because I've never heard him addressed as anything but his name. He cooks, orders groceries, wraps gifts, he doles out directions to the gardener and pool man. He does it all. I suppose he's like the chef and house manager.

Sometimes he comes to my room and lets me know when he's made something sweet. Despite the fact that I'm utterly rotten, sour, and as Mari called me, *bitter*—I have a sweet tooth and Sylvio knows how to sweeten me up, he says.

But the voice that crashes against the door isn't that of the aged Italian man with silver wingtips and too many gold rings.

"Cherry." His voice sounds like money and power, rigid with intention.

"Glenn," I say his name back to him because I'll die a cold, painful death before I answer back sweetly.

"Come down to the kitchen. We're having a family talk."

Family talk. My eyes roll reactively, instinctively as the irony of the phrase makes me bark out a laugh. Family. That's not what we are. He is more of a warden than a stepfather, and he may have loved my mother and I at one time but it's clear that ended the day she died.

"Cherry," he says again, anger throttling his impatience. And even though I'd never admit it, the fierceness in his voice when he gets angry always makes my heart rattle, just a little. "Get the fuck downstairs."

Though he can't see, I roll my eyes again as I throw my legs over the side of the bed, straightening my crumpled dress before standing. Smoothing my hair down, I make my way to the door, but when I pull it open the only trace of Glenn is his cologne.

Downstairs, I find my twenty-seven-year-old stepbrother Max, his twenty-five-year-old brother Conrad, and their father–*my stepfather*–Glenn.

It doesn't matter that I've lived with the three of them for the last fourteen years–they are unfamiliar to me in the most important ways.

Do I know what they smell like, the brand of coffee they prefer, the food they eat, the TV shows they record, the dumb shit they say to one another when they're angry, how much they tip their employees, and how they vote? Yes.

Do I know anything about them, really? No.

Glenn was a widow when he married my mother. I was four when they got married, and five when she was killed. We didn't move, I didn't go stay with some long-lost grandmother. Glenn simply hired someone to live in the house and raise me.

Then, he and his sons went on to live in the same house as if I simply... didn't exist. I was Mari's to raise and that was clear.

"What?" I ask, hands on hips with a defiance so powerful it almost leaves *me* rattled.

Like anyone ignored, their lack of attention or care birthed and nourished a deep hatred inside of me. Around age twelve, I stopped trying to be loved. I hardened. I met their coolness and neglect with anger and insubordination. As time went on, I got worse. I broke rules, I dressed provocatively, I went out, and I came home whenever the fuck I felt like it.

And that fucking heartless asshole didn't even have the nerve to say anything to my face about any of it, either. He told Mari, and made her hand down rules and guidelines. I don't know why that made me hate him more, but it did. Like I wasn't even good enough for his punishment.

"Now that you're eighteen, it's time for you to come to work at the firm."

Max cracks his knuckles, and Conrad drinks from an open can of beer. Glenn stands with his back against the refrigerator door, looking down at his toes.

He's delivering this news like someone died.

Because that's what I am to them—the dark cloud hovering over them reminding everyone of the life they *almost* had. The life where my mother was here and unified us with her love and warmth.

"I don't want to." There I go, sounding like a child stamping her foot. But I can't help it. Believe me when I say

I've tried it all with these three. But nothing gets their attention like my bratty and infuriating rage.

"This isn't a choice." His words escape him despite the fact his jaw seems to stay wired shut, the strain of controlled anger keeping his neck in tight lines.

"I like where I work now." Lies, because who the fuck likes working at a pizza place aside from stoners and old Italian men?

Max snorts, feeding his large hands through his shining dark hair. Glenn's is fading but still, the three of them have the same, bouncing, plentiful waves of luscious soft dark locks. The length is long enough to be wild and sexy when disheveled but not so long as to make any of them look unruly.

"A pizza joint is mentally titilating, huh?"

My eyes pin him down, and everything inside of me screams *look at me when you talk shit to me, coward!* And like he's connected to my thoughts–*Max always seems to know what I'm thinking*–he meets my fuming stare.

"Naa, but a lot of hot guys come in, and it gives me a perfect place to get paid to practice my blowjob skills." My cheeks burn with my bratty comment. I've never blown a guy at *Pizza Castle* and I never fucking would. Still, I can't help the satisfaction soaring through me at the visible displeasure I get from *all three of them.*

"Fucking hell, Cherry. Watch your mouth."

"That's what they say, too," I smile broadly at my stepdad, who is also finally looking at me. They never want to look at me. It used to be maddening. At one point when I was eight, I seriously thought I may be invisible, except that Mari was there–and they saw her so I must be real.

"You can ride with Max and Connie, or me."

My eyes go to my step-brothers, and I watch the solid knot in Conrad's throat jostle up and down as he drinks the last of his beer.

He makes the can look tiny with hands that size.

"I'm not going," I say, not giving up that easily. I know I'll have to do it because even though I'm freshly an adult and have a job, I can't support myself. Not even close. Hell, the money I make at *Pizza Castle* basically pays for my gas and car insurance. Food, rent, and other bills are so fucking out of the question right now.

Unexpectedly, Glenn crosses the room to close the distance between us. My eyes jump to Max and Conrad, who are both watching their father, which makes my pulse rocket.

Glenn wraps his hand around my throat with a terrifying slowness, taking his time to establish that he doesn't have to seize his control quickly—he can move slow and *still* own me.

Gasping, I suck in a defiant breath as his fingertips push down on my throat, my pulse hammering.

"You'll ride with me then." His dark eyes dance between mine, silently daring me to take a stance against him, to raise a question, to claim an offense.

But I lift my hand and wrap it around his, then whisper, *"you'll have to fucking make me."* Before he can process, I fling his hand off my throat, turn around and storm back up to my room.

I've stormed off many times. In my pre-teen years, it was an almost daily habit. No one has ever followed me after the storm-off.

Until today.

No one knocks. Max and Conrad welcome themselves by taking a spot on either side of me on the bed, where I'd just resigned myself to. Max drops a hand to my thigh, and a tingle worms its way up my leg. Conrad matches the movement, and when he fans his fingers over my bare skin, I pull my legs together. On me, the backs of their knuckles graze each other's, and I watch as their eyes meet, holding a brief and silent conversation.

"What do you guys want?" I ask, finding my voice a lot harder to reach with their smooth, vast palms sending waves of warm pleasure up my thighs. They wear different colognes, but they're complementary, and between the touches and scents, I need *out*. I try to stand.

"Stay put," Max advises before drifting his knuckles along his brothers once more.

"You're eighteen now," Conrad supplies in his obliging tone.

Here's the thing about not getting attention from the people who are *supposed* to give it to you: you're fucking *starved* for it, in any capacity. Even if it's fucked up, degrading, toxic, and potentially soul-sucking.

Doesn't matter.

The youth inside of me is famished and these three men are the only thing to put a dent in my voracious appetite to be seen.

"What are you guys doing?" I ask with all the coolness in the fucking world, which I definitely don't feel. Max reaches up and tugs a strand of my long hair. Conrad's hand smooths down then up my thigh. "You guys hate me," I say because they do, and what am I supposed to say? Keeping my shoulders locked in the position of an unphased bad bitch, I force my voice to stay strong.

"What the fuck?"

I know my nipples are hard, and I really fucking hate that I want them because *fuck them*. But also, the primal part of me as a woman cannot deny the feral physical attraction. The evolutionary piece of me sees strong, handsome, intelligent men and screams, "*fuck them! Fuck them!*" It's natural, after all.

But they're withholding and cruel.

And that's *without* unboxing the fact that just a week after I became a legal adult, the three of them had Mari sent back to France.

She told me that was the deal all along. But still, it felt like fucking woman's suffrage, having absolutely zero say in anything in my own life. From the time my mom died until now.

Except *Pizza Castle*. They let me have *Pizza Castle*.

"We want you at the firm, Cherry, so you'll be there." Max smiles as he and Conrad rise in unison.

"And if I don't show up?" I study my cuticles and then the ends of my hair, my sundress undeniably suctioned to my body that is now coated in sweat from having their hands on me. And *liking* it.

I stand, not wanting them to have any advantages over me... as if they don't already.

Conrad steps toward me, resting his hand on my hip, thumb stroking me. My heart does a heavy double thud, making my eyes flash darkness as I calibrate that my stepbrothers just rubbed my legs, and now, one of them is touching my hip... intimately.

"I can wake you up every morning if you need me to." Conrad leans in, his breath hot on my neck, the subtle smell of testosterone burning my nose. Burning *between my legs*. "I can wake you up with a brotherly kiss."

The fuck? My heart slams against my ribs as they simply

turn around and filter out of my room as if all of that were normal... or nothing, even.

I fall to my butt on my bed, head spinning.

What the fuck was that?

And why do I have to be the fucked up little darling who loved it?

Three

I have a best friend. All girls have their one girlfriend, their ride or die, the one who says, "whose car are we taking?" when you tell her you need her help.

But there are some things that are too... *confusing* to share.

Like the fact that the three men I've lived with for years–*the men who claim to be my family yet have not shown up for me a single day in my life*–are suddenly eager to give me their attention.

I didn't say they knew how to give me attention the way I need.

By the looks of them–*and the fact that they are handsome, successful lawyers*–I'd guess they have no problem getting women. I haven't seen one at the house, but have always figured they just didn't want any women knowing where they live.

Apparently, though, their looks get them far enough to skip some core things about what women want. For example, *communication*. As in, *what in the actual fuck is going on, why do they suddenly care, and why did they just have their hands on my thighs and...* Fuck. I'm so confused.

I may have a silver spoon up my ass, or whatever bullshit people say about kids that grow up with money like I did, but I have a miserable existence. And I'd give up everything for a minute of something real.

I give myself five seconds to freak out, then after, I make a fucking plan to stay strong.

If they think they're going to intimidate me, *they can fucking think again.*

A week later, Glenn had an entire room full of women's work suits sent to our house, and today, it's my first day at the firm.

The Law Offices of Glenn Mason and Sons.

Satan and his Spawn so aptly own the place. Allegedly, Max and Conrad *earned* their keep on that business name, but it smells like nepotism-drenched designer suits if you ask me.

There have been no more run-ins with those two since the day in my bedroom. In fact, they'd gone back to not even acknowledging my presence if we were in a room at the same time. It was starting to make me wonder if I had fucking pathetically fantasized the entire thing.

Until now.

Max's hand falls on my waist from behind as he reaches across me to the French Press. He's the tallest of the three of them, around six-foot-five. His eyes are set a bit farther apart than Conrad's, and rather than the clean-shaven look his younger brother and father abide by, Max has a chin coated in scruff. Kempt, of course, but nonetheless, a bit rugged and *a lot* sexy.

"Pencil skirts look good on you." His voice is raspy, like the morning cobwebs are still there, and it's sexy. All men sound sexy when they first wake up; it's something about them in their most primal state that gets me going. *It's not Max; it's the situation*, I tell myself.

"Pencil skirts look good on everyone." I actually do believe that. But arguing with Satan's sexy spawn is in my DNA, apparently.

His hand leaves me, and then he and his brother are out the door, Conrad not even meeting my eyes. They may actually make me crazy. It's so fucking hot and cold.

I pour the coffee into my tumbler and twist on the lid. When I turn, I'm face to face with my stepdad.

I have few memories of him from when I was really young. I think the trauma of losing my mom jumbled my mind some because those first years we were all together are kind of gone from my brain as toddler-age memories tend to do, with the exception of some fuzzy flashbacks.

But I *do* remember Glenn.

I remember his warm smile and his soft hands and the way he held me on his hip while he stirred sauce on the stove. It smelled like oregano or spices of some kind, and the air was warm and sticky with homemade food and love. Mom was laughing on the other side of the kitchen, and she had flour on her clothes. She was wearing a blue blouse with white daisies, I remember that, too.

Everything else was a blur, but I will never forget *the feeling* of being loved.

Now I don't know if that version of Glenn simply doesn't exist, or if my childhood mind is misremembering everything to protect me.

It doesn't feel that way, though.

That's why his emotional neglect and complete lack of interest in me as a human hurt so much. He *did* love me.

He blinks. "What are you thinking about?" His voice is so rough and raspy, too, like his son's. Only... rougher like his ship has seen more torrid and wild seas than the others. My mouth goes dry.

He looks good in a suit, and I've never been able not to notice that. This morning, though, I let my eyes trek across the terrain of his broad chest. I bet women love running their fingers down the rippled split of his pecs, tracing his nipple, then dragging their nails over his tanned skin.

"What am I doing at your firm?" I ask, focusing on making my face seriously unimpressed. My pussy pulses as my eyes do another pass of him wrapped in that sharp black suit. I don't think he's ever asked me what I was thinking about... like, ever.

"Personal secretary to the partners."

I cock an eyebrow. "So, an obedient little fetcher to you, Max, and Connie?"

He comes toward me, his alpha domineering energy encircling me, making my temples pound. "I've never heard you call Conrad by his nickname."

I have the biggest urge to be bratty. And with his eyes on me, his presence eating up mine, I have the confidence to do it.

"It sounds better, don't you think? Listen." I step into his aura, my heart tripping up at my sudden boldness. Usually, my idea of bratty is picking fights and stomping around but this... this is *a lot,* even for me. "Thanks for the ride, *Connie.*" I draw out the name, purring it, and Glenn's dark eyes fall to my mouth.

"Get in the car."

I don't even have the decency to hide the smirk that comes with irritating Glenn. And I do my very best to worm my way under his skin on the drive through town–turning the satellite radio to the most annoying pop music I can find–*thanks 2000s throwback station.* When he turns it down, I turn it back up. When he's shirked that off, I put my heeled foot in the center of the dashboard, using my tongue and my thumb to wipe away the scuffs left from the gravel drive. He tells me to get my foot off the dash, and I do–when I'm done cleaning my heels.

I don't know why his silent treatment on the drive irritates me. I guess I thought with him making me work at his firm that the fourteen years of ignoring me would come to an end. I should be so angry to have been pushed off on a French nanny that I don't even care about his attention, love, and focus.

But like I said, *I want it.* The little girl inside me wants it. And despite the fact that I hate them, loathe them, despise them for their ability to essentially ignore a little girl–I can't deny the biological reaction they elicit from me.

Tall with strong frames and disciplined physiques, dark eyes that captivate even a stranger, pressed suits, and brains too full for their own good. Any woman would be attracted.

I shouldn't be since Glenn loved my mother.

I shouldn't be because I grew up in the same home with Max and Conrad.

No, we didn't skip rope, share Xbox controllers, pop popcorn over a campfire, and hide under the bed together during storms. Even though our childhood engagement was more like Cinderella with her evil step-sisters, I can't ignore that I've grown up with them. I remember their awkward teenage phases, with acne and braces.

Still, the distance they'd put between them and me made them feel more like strangers than family.

I hated that fact growing up.

Thinking about Max and Conrad with their hands on my thigh as I suck up all of Glenn's cologne in the luxury SUV... I don't hate that fact anymore.

But now, as things between us are clearly shifting with Mari gone, I plan to be in control of what happens next.

Two weeks of working in the office go by quickly because I stay busy. Believing I was going to be tasked with picking up dry cleaning and getting coffees, I actually don't do any of that shit.

Glenn pairs me with a paralegal on my very first day, and immediately I begin learning how to read legal briefs. Seems simple, right? Reading something. Well, legal briefs may as well be written in Japanese because they're completely foreign to me. After two weeks, I have a trusty spreadsheet of terms and jargon made so that I can read my first brief on my own at some point.

I didn't expect to learn or even be put in a role where learning was on the menu. But here I am, and to my surprise, I'm loving it.

As I'm filing paperwork with just a handful of minutes left in my workday, Justin, another paralegal in the office, approaches me.

I've noticed that everyone at The Law Offices of Glenn Mason and Sons is... good looking.

Justin is no different, though he's a stark difference from the Mason men. Blonde hair combed in a preppy coif, navy blue suit pressed like he's about to deliver a speech to the White House, blue eyes staying on mine like a gentleman.

I can't help but wonder, do gentlemen work for snakes? The Mason men are snakes. They have to be because the idea that they were just unusually cruel *to me* is something my fragile heart can't take.

Everyone here at the firm may treat the Masons like they walk on water... They might even boast that they're the "best bosses" they've ever had but... come on, they *have* to say that.

What are they gonna do, talk shit about the people who sign their paychecks?

"Cherry," he greets me using my name, and I'm pretty sure all men love my name because it makes them think of pie. Warm, sweet, tasty, and comforting... that's what they want me to be with a name like Cherry.

"Hey there, Justin," I greet him with a smile, though no part of me feels like putting on the Cherry Pie persona that every man is so fucking hungry for.

From the corner of my eye, I see Max talking with another lawyer and two associates. His neck is full of strain; his broad chest tipped over the desk, knuckles braced against the wood, propping himself up as he doles out orders or reprimands; it's hard to tell.

"You have any plans for this weekend?" Justin asks, the *thurthurthur* of his index finger dragging across the tabbed files grabbing my focus from Max.

"Not really," I say with a smile. Truthfully, most of my weekends had been spent with Mari and her friends. She was in a circle of nannies and au pairs here in California that met twice a month for brunch or cocktails, or whatever. She brought me with her, and even though I was technically an outsider, I never felt like I belonged anywhere more.

He wiggles a manila folder until it's broken through the wall of folders, and with a gentle shove, he slides it in with the rest. "I'd love to take you out for coffee, I mean, if you're not seeing anyone."

For some reason, I glance at Max again. and I don't know why I give it any thought. but he's gone...I can't help but wonder where he went.

"Um, sure," I reply absentmindedly.

"Sure you're seeing someone?" Justin's fingers come

dangerously close to mine, but my heart doesn't speed up. My stomach doesn't tip. My pussy doesn't flutter.

Justin should make me feel *all the things* that the love songs promise.

After all, he's kind, on the way to having a prestigious career, sweet enough, and handsome. He looks more like a Ken doll than anyone I've ever met.

But all I can feel is the anxious twist in my gut chanting *where is Max, where is Max.*

"I'm not seeing anyone, no." I smooth my palms over my hair, checking for flyaways. I'm not used to wearing my hair in a professional chignon. "Coffee sounds nice."

Justin's grin is all white teeth and sweetness. I match it, but it's completely forced. "What's your number, Cherry?"

We exchange numbers on the back of a Mason and Sons business card. I slip it into my bag, and when it's time to leave an hour later, Justin is already gone when Glenn comes to collect me.

While I gather my things, he stands with his hands in his pockets at the elevators, staring at his feet as he waits silently for me to join. As I approach, the doors pull open and I walk straight inside.

We ride it down to the parking garage in silence. We drive home in complete silence and my confusion over how I feel about these assholes keeps me from being bratty.

Before opening my door once we're home, Glenn speaks. "Less fraternizing. You'll never be successful at the firm if you're flirting with coworkers. It's unprofessional."

Then he goes inside the house like the self-righteous, selfish asshole he is.

But no. I am *not* letting him do this shit to me anymore.

I storm inside after him.

Four

Somehow, Satan's sexy spawns have beat us home. Then again, being a rich, hunky asshole probably allows them to do virtually anything they want, like blow red lights with no repercussions. They've lived their entire lives that way so far; why stop now?

I ignore them and their sexily loosened ties hanging limply around their necks as they pick at a tray of fresh vegetables, talking quietly back and forth. I ignore how their eyes seem to gravitate to their dad and myself like they know the spark is ignited, and the wick is only so long.

"*Excuse me?*"

Fuck, okay, I'm normally wittier than this but ever since two weeks back when Max and Conrad made me feel... *good*... I can't seem to get my head right. Even now. I keep my eyes tamped down on Satan in the suit because a random glance at either of my two step-brothers has the potential to reroute my brain completely.

Glenn shimmies out of his suit jacket, draping it over the

kitchen island as he begins loosening his cuff links. Sylvio filters in, arms full of items presumably for dinner.

"Masons, hello," he says kindly, immediately getting to work as if all four of us aren't there. As if all four of us being in the *same room together* actually talking to one another isn't a fucking Christmas miracle. But it is.

"Sylvio, how are you?" Conrad asks as he pops a cherry tomato into his mouth.

And that's it. The casual greeting to Sylvio is the final fucking straw. Who knew it would take so little? But after years of this and without Mari by my side, I've fucking had enough.

"You can't hire someone to raise me, ignore me my entire life, and then expect me to follow any fucking rules or guidance or advice from you; you realize that, right?" The chignon decides to break free, and as sweat forms on my back, my long hair topples down behind me. "I wasn't fraternizing, *Glenn*. Justin approached me. *He* asked *me* out. He asked me if I wanted to get coffee. I said yes."

He won't meet my gaze, and I won't fucking have it. I charge into his space, and I can see how much control it takes for him to stay there and not turn away from me like I'm a poisonous thorn in his side. Our eyes lock. My pulse races. I take his chin, which is starting to grow rough as afternoon bleeds into evening.

Jerking his face down to mine, holding his chin like the hero would normally grab his heroine, I smile at him.

"Don't you dare try to parent me now, *daddy*," I say, the word an ugly hiss, not a term of pseudo-sexual enjoyment.

With the courage of his silence, I face my other aggressors. "And next time, have the balls to finish what you start," I say to them, knowing they know *exactly* what I'm referring to.

And finally, they're silent by *my choice*, not because of theirs.

The smile on my lips as I head upstairs is probably the biggest in my life.

I don't get butterflies when Justin and I text. Maybe they'll come and it's just too soon. Maybe I need to attract them by putting out butterfly bait.

An hour before our date, I roll perfume behind my ears, along my wrist, and even some between my thighs, in case things go *that* well. I wear my hair down and straight because it's different from the bun or chignon I wear at work. I add red lipstick and mascara before I put on my favorite black sundress with the ties on the shoulders and the ruffle along the short hem.

I didn't want Justin to pick me up at my house. He didn't mention knowing that Glenn Mason is my stepfather, and since my mother was only married to him for a year, she never got around to changing my name. And though he legally *was* my parent, he didn't change my surname either.

I'm still Cherry Halford.

Glenn, Max, and Conrad are perched around the kitchen island, half-empty pints of beer and papers scattered everywhere. They work together like that all the time. Until recently, I didn't so much as garner a glance from them if I passed through. Mari always reassured me it wasn't for lack of care but rather their *need* to focus.

Big smart men with their big brains. God forbid they spare an hour of their time to make someone feel like a human.

I didn't get mad at Mari for her efforts. She was a peacekeeper through and through. Maybe that's why things have suddenly shifted in this house? Mari was keeping us all separate but peaceful. In her absence, I have no one keeping me from lashing out.

Maybe it's time I get it all off my chest.

Thirty minutes later, I'm parked at a coffee house next to a Globo Fitness. We decided to meet in the next town over, and while I knew why *I* didn't want to meet in town, I was starting to wonder why Justin didn't.

But I'm not looking to be wifed up anytime soon, so a few red flags won't ruin this date. I just want to laugh and maybe fool around a little. My last fling was with the manager at *Pizza Castle*, a twenty-nine-year-old college drop-out named Charlie, who became somewhat obsessed with me after our singular date. And by date, I definitely mean fuck-fest against the closed ovens one night after everyone had gone, and I was feeling particularly horny.

As much as I hated relinquishing the job that was my choice, a part of me was glad to walk away from Charlie. It did feel like I was potentially one more dead-air phone call away from being the focus of a true-crime podcast.

"I'll go with a doppio espresso." Handing my card to the barista, she runs it and passes it back before I step aside into the grove of caffeine-hungry people waiting for their fix. After getting my drink, I find a two-person table in the center of the coffeehouse and take a seat, waiting anxiously for Justin.

From here, I have a perfect view of the parking lot. I watch for thirty-nine minutes as moms holding the wrists of their small children hustle in for an extra hit of energy. I smile at a group of elderly people coming to do Bible study at the long table centering the coffeehouse. And I give hello nods to those coming in on dates, passing shy smiles to one another as they awkwardly wait in line, not knowing what to say or do.

And then, after giving him another ten minutes, I get back

into my car, wired off two shots of premium espresso, and drive home.

When I went out before, I told Mari. I'd either stop by her room or shoot her a text. Sometimes–*though rarely*–I'd leave her a note. It would give me a chance to practice my French.

Without her, I have no one who even cares about my whereabouts, and that is part of the reason why I'm completely fucking shocked to come home to find Satan and his spawn glaring, seething, all six fists curled.

"Jesus, what crawled up your asses?" I only regard them for a minute before hanging my purse on the hook near the door and going for a sparkling water in the fridge. Planning to slide up the back staircase to my room, I'm surprised to be stopped.

Face colliding with a wall of chest; I look up to find my sweating can of sparkling water has left wet marks on Max's t-shirt. His lip is curled like a wild dog ready to tear into his prey.

"You tell us when you're leaving and where you're going." His tone makes goosebumps rise up on my skin, but I simply lift my chin and purse my lips in playful defiance, as if his act has no effect on me.

Pulling my phone from my back pocket, I wiggle it in front of his face, attempting to cut the tension between us. "It's called a phone. If you gave a shit, you could call. But I'm guessing after not caring, oh, I don't know, *my entire life* that you guys don't actually care tonight. So get off my ass."

Glenn shoves away from the kitchen island so forcefully that the metal barstool skitters against the floor, and before I can process, he's gone, leaving a trail of quiet curse words in his wake.

Conrad is now at my side, but the way he's looking down at me mirrors Max's disposition.

"Excuse me, I've literally been on tons of dates, and no one gave a shit before." My nipples poke through my sundress as their hot exhales flank me.

Conrad's hand takes mine in a soft pinch. "Forty-six. You've been on forty-six dates, including all the times you stayed at that fucking hole-in-the-wall and ate cold pizza with Charlie or Devin."

I'm in the process of recessing back, shock and disgust on my face when Max takes my other hand. I try to pull both of my hands free, but their grip tightens, their cologne and traces of beer breath hugging me like a drug-induced fog.

"We cared about you, but Mari cared *for* you better than we ever could, Cherry," Max says, and the flush that rolls through me is hard to hide. Conrad's eyes fall to my exposed collarbone, and he groans a little, a strand of his dark hair falling across his forehead as he tips his head to take me in. Max does the same, and I stop trying to pull my hands free. I let them study me; I grow stronger as their eyes traverse my curves, all the way from my calves up to the slope of my bare neck.

"Mari was the only person who ever cared about *or* for me," I finally manage to say, my voice coming out uncharacteristically weak.

Then, as if they'd rehearsed it, they release my hands in silent unison. Max shakes his head, still so intently focused on me that I grow antsy on my feet, shifting in my espadrilles like I need to pee.

"Sometimes you can care about a person too much." Max's eyes search mine as I look to Conrad, who meets me with the same searching.

"And distance is the only thing that keeps everyone safe," Conrad finishes his brother's thought.

"So," I draw out, refusing to get sucked into their charisma and tall, dark, and handsome schtick. I'm turned on by their sheer proximity but that's only because they are so foreign to me, my brain doesn't register that I shouldn't want them. "You ignored and neglected me for years to keep us *all* safe, huh?"

Max licks his lips as he stares at mine. Conrad looks at his brother, then me.

"You live in an estate most people will never even visit, much less live in. You have had anything you've ever wanted. Unlimited resources. The best schooling. Anything you've wanted, you've had," Conrad says flatly.

Though neither are soft, Conrad is usually the less harsh of the two satanic spawn.

"Money doesn't buy happiness," I retort, though I'm not pleased with how basic it is. I expect more from myself when it comes to bratty quips, but they have me on my toes lately. Scrambled and confused.

"Clearly, since we're all miserable," Max says.

"You two are miserable?" I question with sarcastic surprise.

"All four of us have been miserable." Conrad smooths the backs of his knuckles down the length of my arm before adding, "But that ends now."

And before I can ask, balk, refuse, or sass... they're gone, heading up the stairs to their part of the house.

I'm left horny, confused, and hugely intrigued.

Justin ghosting me is the last thing on my mind when I fall asleep.

Five

I don't see Satan or his spawn the rest of the weekend. On Sunday evening, I finally run into Glenn when I'm making myself the last frozen batch of pasta Mari prepared before she left.

I'd be lying if I said I didn't think about what Max and Conrad had said to me Friday night for nearly every moment thereafter. I did.

Thinking and rethinking everything has gotten me absolutely nowhere.

"Smells good," Glenn offers as he drifts around the kitchen behind me. Sylvio prepares everything for the three of them—that's always been the case. Mari and I usually made our own meals—she taught me how to cook.

"It will be," I reply, offering no *in* to conversation. If Satan feels bad about anything that's happened, he can tell me. After all, from my vantage point, things are very one-sided. I didn't ignore them. I didn't ask for this life.

"Mari's?" he asks as if he doesn't know it's hers. But if Conrad knew how many dates I'd ever gone on (and if you think I didn't stay up half the night counting in my head if indeed that figure was accurate, think again). If they have cared at a distance the way they've alluded to caring, there's no way that Glenn doesn't know Mari and I had stockpiled the freezer with all of my favorites before she left the country.

I drop the slotted spoon onto the cooktop and spin to face him, sick of the ambiguity. I'm so full of hurt and anger that simply pretending the last fourteen years didn't go down the way they did just doesn't fucking work for me.

"Seriously? Are you *seriously* asking that?"

It's the first time I've seen him since Friday when I came back from my non-date. He's wearing gray sweats and a white v-neck t-shirt. For a moment, I get a flash of thirty-one-year-old Glenn lifting me up to pluck the ripest of peaches from the tree. It's been so long since I've let myself revisit those memories–the few that are left. I shake it from my brain as I assume the position to argue–*hands braced to my hips.*

"Of course, it's Mari's. Because before she left, we cooked for two weeks to fill this freezer with comfort food for me."

"Why do you need comfort food?" he asks, his eyes moving over my body the same way his spawn did just two days ago.

"Are you fucking kidding me?"

This man is a lawyer. No, he isn't just a lawyer. He's *the fucking boss,* the owner, the executive in chief. And he's seriously asking why I would need comfort food? Closing the distance between us until our bare feet are toe-to-toe, I have to work very fucking hard to control my temper as I respond to his idiocracy.

"Mari came into my life one week after my mother died. And one week after I legally became an adult, you stole *her* from me, too. I'm a human being, not some fucking robot without feelings. I need comfort for my losses!"

He studies me, and as the stretch of quiet between us lengthens, the angrier I become. Hot tears bubble up behind my eyes, but I refuse to cry. At least not in front of the man who has caused the tears.

"Too?"

I shake my head. "What?"

His expression morphs into sad confusion. "You said, *you stole her from me, too*. Which means you think I stole someone else from you."

My heart races. These are things I've never shared with anyone, not Mari, not girlfriends, no one. Not even the pathetic guidance counselor who ached to have me pour my guts out.

The thing is, though, how does one man become widowed twice? Seems awfully strange, doesn't it? I can't muster up any memories of Glenn and my mother arguing, of him ever even raising his voice to her. But I was young when they met. My last memories of them together–*us together*–I was only five. How can I accurately remember much less have understood what I saw back then? My memory is unreliable.

I can hardly breathe when he reaches out and brushes hair off my face, behind my shoulder. "Who else did I take from you, Cherry?"

I attempt to swallow but a knot is in my throat, and it's hard to breathe through my nose because all I can smell is him. His strangely comforting scent. Why does it comfort me? I don't know, but somehow, it does. And it only serves to confuse me even more.

With his thumb and curled knuckles, he pinches my chin. My face floods with heat, searing down my neck, into my torso, spreading like wildfire through my limbs.

"Mom," I say unbelievably because I didn't ever think I'd

have the guts to voice my deepest secret fear. Not without reason or evidence, at least.

His eyes study my mouth, his chest rising and falling so noticeably slow that a tingle forms between my thighs. "I loved your mother very much." He says, and it's not the defense I was expecting. "But you're right. If she hadn't met me, she'd probably still be here."

The water boils over onto the reduction cooktop with a sizzle.

"What?" I question because I wasn't expecting that answer. Hell, I wasn't expecting anything to change between any of us ever. In truth, I figured one day I'd move out, or they'd move and leave me here. I guess. I don't know.

One more small step and we're closer than we've been in *actual year*s. Since I was just a little girl.

He doesn't answer the question, but instead questions me, "Do you think I've kept you at arm's length all this time because I hate you, Cherry? Is that why you think I've been cold and disconnected?"

My mouth goes dry and my lips stick together as I force out once more, "what?"

I step back but he steps forward, reaching up to rest his hand against the hood above the range. His sharpened, dark gaze stays locked onto my blue eyes as he reaches behind me, tapping the induction cooktop to turn off the boiling pasta.

His chest connects with my shoulder as he does, and though it's just a few seconds of connection, my reaction is undeniably rattling. My palms glaze over in sweat, my spine goes wobbly, and the flutter in my pussy is all consuming.

"Answer me."

"Yes," I manage because standing here like a breathless fool in front of my step-dad is not happening. "Yes, I do. Because you don't ignore someone you love." Then, proud of myself for mustering it through the confusing haze of lust, I add, "*you don't ignore a child.*"

"I've never hated you," he says, stepping away, giving me room to breathe and think. His proximity was maddening for a few weird moments. "I was detached for a few years, for a variety of reasons, but I'm here now."

I turn away from him and turn the stove back on. I catch my breath. "Yes, because that's how parenting works. You can tap out for years and then tap back in, whenever you feel like it, no matter how much emotional damage you've already done."

He touches the back of my arm but I yank it away. "Don't touch me," I hiss, my eyes burning with anger, hurt, and fear. Because I *want* him to care. It's not too late. Only now, I don't need a dad–I *need* praise and worship, I need to be shown that *I am important* and that *I deserve love*. But I'm afraid he can't do that, and the role he wants to fill just isn't there anymore.

I'm grown up. It's too late.

"I don't need a father anymore. I needed that for the last fourteen years but not anymore. I'm an adult now."

"I don't want to be your father, Cherry," he says, the back of his hand smoothing down my arm from behind me. My eyelids flutter closed as all the air rushes from my diaphragm on a heated exhale. "The silver lining in my bad choices is that you're both the little girl I loved and a complete stranger. One I want to take care of in every fucking way possible."

Right when I want him to step up and touch me, give me more of him, of these heady admissions... he steps back.

"Have a nice night, Cherry."

And he disappears, leaving me wanting him more than I ever have, in ways that I never have.

Six

The drive to the office Monday morning is extremely fucking awkward. All I can think about is what Glenn said to me in the kitchen last night. Not just what he said but how sure he was saying it. Each word spoken with confidence, not a mustered one, but one that came from longevity.

Like maybe he felt that way for a while... like he said.

The thought that Glenn Mason is not the villain of my story is jarring. I've never considered it before because the fact remains–mom's not here, he's a twice-widower, and my step-brothers don't have their mother either.

I don't need to be a fucking detective to know that the entire thing smells fishy.

And while I've never had many conversations around or desire to know my father, there's the fact that he's nowhere to be found. Dead, perhaps. Not that I remember him—and that fact also means maybe I never knew him.

More startling than my willingness to keep an open mind

about his explanations, whenever I do get to hear them, is how little I care that this man watched me grow up.

We would be frowned upon.

No one would understand step-brothers pleasing their step-sister. The world would hate a step-father *loving* his step-daughter. Though he legally *was* my guardian, and yes he did watch me transition from spandex bike shorts and scrunchies to bralettes and yoga pants, he didn't have an active role in any of it.

Passive, that's what he's always been to me.

Until now, and something tells me that dirty-mouthed aggressive Glenn is a man I'd like.

"Cherry," Glenn breaks the silence as he pulls his black SUV into the parking garage beneath the firm.

"Glenn," I respond because I know that annoys him. And after everything he said to me last night–he left. He left when I needed more of him, so fuck him. He'll have to work harder than a lousy two-liner in the parking garage before work.

He parks the vehicle and while still belted in, turns to face me. "I meant every word I said last night but I realize this is coming out of nowhere." His eyes don't shy away from mine, as if he's not nervous at all, and holy shit does his confidence turn me on. "I'm giving you time to process what I told you. What I want."

I lean in, popping my post-coffee gum. My lips are merely an inch from his when I say, "you expect me to believe I'm all you want and yet, I'm unhappy." I lean back and blow another bubble, popping it. "Real men keep their women happy, don't they?" Satisfied with the way his face floods with anger, I hop out of the SUV and get lucky as a group of paralegals are walking up to the elevators. Joining them, I peer over my shoulder to see Glenn at the back of his SUV, fists clenched at his sides, his dark eyes almost black.

Two hours later, I'm finally looking up for a moment to check the time when my heart jumps into my throat.

I'm up on my feet, running in my heels toward Justin as soon as I see him. His face is an ombre of purples and deep reds, along his eye socket and jaw. As I approach, hands out, he raises his arm to me, telling me not to touch him. I halt in my tracks.

"Justin, what happened?" I hiss in a whisper because his body language is private and guarded as he huddles toward the file cabinets, head hung low.

Conrad knew exactly how many dates I'd been on. They knew, *all three of them.*

I press my hand to my forehead. "Justin, oh my god, I'm so sorry, I had no idea—"

He cuts me off in an angry whisper so potent that veins bulge at his temples. "Why the fuck didn't you tell me who your father is? Seriously, Cherry. It's one thing to be a tease but to put my job at risk?"

I jerk back. "A tease? How was I ever a tease?"

Justin smooths a palm down his face, trying to regain composure. Sweat appears on his upper lip, and suddenly, I am full of hate for Justin.

"Listen Cherry, I was just looking to have some fun. Date, casually," he says, smoothing a hand over the top of his hair before peering around me to see if anyone is watching. "I didn't know Glenn Mason was your father."

"He's not my father," I counter, but why, I don't know. No, Glenn isn't my father but what am I fighting for? To keep Justin? The guy who's terrified by other men, because what? He got a little black eye and likes his job? A job that he could get a million other places, I might add.

Justin is not worth the fight.

Justin snaps to attention and whatever focus I'd earned from him dissolves completely when Max's voice drifts over my shoulder.

"Cherry, get in here."

I turn, not giving Justin another thought.

"Get in here?" I question. "That's how you talk to everyone or just me?"

He rolls his eyes. "Please come in, Cherry." He fights it, but I see a smile.

I go because what choice do I have, and honestly, I'm interested to see what they have to say for themselves. Though I'll have to do some acting because in truth, *fuck Justin*. He got what he deserved.

"Which one of you did it?" I ask, hands on hips, surveying the private office. Glenn rests behind his desk, looking like a god, Conrad is perched on the couch adjacent to his father's desk, and Max stands next to me.

I look at Glenn, then Conrad, and then Max. And then I do it again. Finally, Glenn nods to Conrad, and like he's been queued, Conrad rises from the couch, coming to my other side.

Glenn's voice finds us as their hands' stroke down my arms and along my shoulders. I want to protest, but they smell *good* and my skin is ablaze, and *I'm only fucking human*.

"You can't be angry with us, Cherry. This is life when you're ours."

"Ours," I repeat, my core ripe with heat and need as Conrad's fingers sieve through my hair, Max smoothing his palm down the length of my spine.

"We'll give you some time, but there will be no *Justins*

while we wait."

My head spins with his dizzying admission. *Their* admission, I think. "The three of you?" I ask, feeling like I'm a minute behind.

"We're a package deal," Glenn gruffs, and then he just sits there, eyes trained on me as his sons begin my disrobing.

My blouse is carefully removed over my head, and my pencil skirt is unzipped before it's lowered. I'm left in panties, a bra, my high heels, and thigh high stockings, and before I have a chance to calibrate, Max and Conrad are pressing my hands to their stiff groins.

"You're beautiful, Cherry, and a person like *Justin* can't appreciate you the way you deserve," Glenn continues.

I like the sound of that.

Zippers descend, and my palms are filled with hot, hard cocks as my head tips back, two tongues sliding down the column of my neck.

"*Justin* wants to see your tits, Cherry. He won't make you come," Glenn continues as his sons' hands roam all over my belly and breasts. A moment later, my bra sails to my feet.

Max's dark eyes take mine in a silent moment of permission, which I grant with a breathy exhale. Slowly he aligns his lips with my nipple then suckles at my bare breast, his brother's mouth locked onto a spot of soft skin behind my ear. I don't know who, but one of them is sweeping his fingers through my sticky slit, leaving my panties drenched.

Holy shit. This. Feels. Good.

"Most men are like Justin, Cherry. They want you for themselves, for their *own* pleasure," Glenn says, and when Conrad stops kissing my neck, I tip my head forward to find Glenn's eyes.

Conrad takes my other breast into his mouth, Max still

sucking and biting, tenderly at the first.

"We want you for *your* pleasure. Anything that comes with it is just a perk." Glenn leans forward, letting his eyes take in his sons feasting on my full, naked tits before looking at me again. "Anything you want or need, and we *will* be the men that give it to you."

I don't know if he means only sex or life? I don't know if he means forever.

I don't know anything, and at this moment, I don't *want* to know anything.

I just don't want *this* to stop.

Conrad's voice is soft and tender. "Get on your hands and knees for us, beautiful."

Without needing to be asked twice, I get on the ground, keeping my chin held high so as to not break eye contact with Glenn.

Max kneels before me, his cock speared in front of him, red and veiny, thick and solid. He pumps himself, foreskin sliding back to reveal a perfect pink crown, the slit wide, pooling with precome.

"You want to look at Dad?" Max asks me. He nods back to his brother then Conrad takes control of my hips, shifting me so that I can see Glenn better while Max positions himself at my face.

Conrad's fingers spread me open, my wetness audible as he does. "She's ready," he says, his voice low and raspy, more like Max's.

Max cups my cheek. "Open your mouth and get what *I know* you want."

Smoothing his hands along my bare ass, Conrad spreads me open once more, his cockhead pressing against my cunt. "You want love, and that's all we want to do. *Love* you."

Their hips begin moving in unison. With a gasp and jolt, Conrad's cock fills me, and Max plugs my throat. My eyes veer back to Glenn, who is watching with a libidinous smirk. Restraint tugs his jaw as his broad chest heaves with controlled *excitement*.

Max threads his fingers in my hair while slowly pumping his hips, fucking my mouth both gently and erotically. Conrad's fingers coil into my hips as he saws his meaty cock in and out of me, groaning with each stroke.

My entire body feels weightless and warm, and I realize as Max's salty flesh impales me with more force and Conrad's cock sinks deep into me that this is what I've been missing.

Being worshiped and adored.

I'm sure a therapist could make a lot of money off me. But all I've wanted is love and it certainly feels like it's closer than ever before.

Unanswered questions drift easily to the back of my mind as Conrad's breathing intensifies rapidly.

"Come for them," Glenn commands. *"Come for my boys."*

A strand of his silvering hair falls across his eyes, his strong hand batting it back. The hand that I can imagine smoothing across my collarbone, holding the back of my neck while he recklessly fucks me.

His gaze is my undoing.

"There she goes," Conrad grunts, hollowing me only to sink back inside, hard and fast. He holds himself there as my cunt spasms, milking him for every single molecule of pleasure I can. Max's grip on my head softens, his fingers spanning tenderly over my scalp as he holds himself on my tongue, ribbons of come coating the back of my throat in pulsing, rhythmic waves.

I find myself leaning back toward Conrad, loving the

flutter of his orgasm tearing through me, needing more. Max tips forward, following my mouth, still holding me gently as his orgasm comes to an end.

I swallow everything he gives me, and when Conrad pulls out and dribbles down my thigh, I hate the loss.

I blink through the haze to find Glenn looking both starving and sated. "Good girl," he says, before turning his focus back to his iPad.

Max helps me up, and I find Conrad already put away and at my side, belt buckled. He holds my face and seals our mouths together in a long, slow kiss. Can't he taste his brother? The way he murmurs delightful moans into my mouth tells me he does and likes it. Max kisses me next and it's just as slow and torturous.

They dress me, finger comb my hair, blot the sweat from my brow, and Conrad even uses Kleenex to clean up my pussy. Their aftercare–while silent–is... impeccable.

I feel all the things I've always yearned to feel.

Seen, taken care of, and loved.

"Let's get you something to eat and get you back to your desk, okay?" Conrad says, smoothing his fingers down the lapel of my blouse, eyes dancing between mine.

And then he does.

The rest of the day is a blur. Kinda like how they portray car accident survivors on TV shows–jumpy but speechless. That was me for the remaining five hours of the work day. I ate lunch with some of the paralegals, nodding and smiling along all while trying to process what had happened hours earlier.

And how good it felt.

Glenn's permissive eyes, his coaxing energy—all of it was too fucking hot.

Max and Conrad's hands all over me, their cocks stuffing

me while their silky words wrapped around me. They wanted to fill me with love, and as stupid as it all sounds now post-orgasm, the sentiment is still inside me.

They do want me, all three of them.

They have explaining to do. I won't let them off the hook for their past behavior either. But the attraction, the comfort, the sparks—it all exists with them.

No one grows up thinking they're going to fuck the man that loved their mother and be fucked by his evil offspring, especially not me. I grew up hating them from afar–yet we were all physically so close to one another the entire time.

The walk to the SUV in the parking garage is quiet. As soon as our doors close, Glenn tips his head back against the headrest and lets loose a shuddering groan.

"Cherry, you're going to fucking kill me."

"Excuse me?" My heart races excitedly and nervously, like I'm about to run a race I'm not sure I can win. But I sure as hell want to try.

He doesn't respond but his grip on the steering wheel is scarily tight.

As soon as I'm home, I take a long, hot shower.

The tinge of lingering guilt I felt about today seemed to evaporate in that shower. Because when I got out with a hungry stomach, I had a smile on my face.

You know what? I can be a good person and be kinda fucked in the head if it means I'm happy, right? Who does my happiness really harm?

No one.

Dressing for dinner in nothing but my satin robe–*which I've never gone downstairs in before*–I head downstairs with a poker face, determined to get answers before falling headfirst into something I probably won't survive should I want to quit.

Seven

That night I came downstairs in my satin robe, I had plans to be bratty but Glenn decided to not give me the chance. He took the cake for fucking asshole as soon as I entered the room.

He gave me one look, turned back to his iPad and said, "go change into something appropriate."

I stomped my foot. "I'll wear what I want, *Glenn*."

Without a glance at my mini-tantrum, he kept his focus on his work. *At least that's the Glenn I know*, I think to myself. "Don't put yourself on display like a cheap whore, especially when we employ staff."

From his spot at the sink peeling potatoes, I spoke to said staff. "Sylvio, can you deal only with Glenn tonight? I'm going to be dressed like a whore and Glenn is scared for you."

He broke his whistling long enough to say, "sure thing," then returned to his task. Because no one wants to ruffle the feathers of the Mason men.

That's the only thing I care about doing.

"Go change for Dad, Cherry. Be a good girl," Conrad coaxes, his voice affectionate and tender.

But I wanted to fight. Casting a broad smile to each of them, I pulled the tie on my robe like a ripcord to a fucking parachute. The mauve satin floated to my ankles and I stood there, completely naked.

"I don't belong to the three of you and you don't tell me what I can and can't do."

Then I sat at the dinner table and waited.

We ate in silence. Sylvio prepared steaks to our preferences, green beans sauteed in garlic, and potatoes with parmesan and parsley. A lot of dinner required a knife, and a knife yields a lot of back and forth... *jiggling*. Needless to say, they didn't get up from the table like gentlemen when I stood to leave.

That was a few days ago, and since then, Conrad has kissed me in the hallway, Max has rubbed my shoulders while we waited for our coffee, and Glenn has stocked the freezer with foods *closely* paralleling what Mari and I made before she left.

But still.

None of us have spoken so much as a hello. Even on the commute yesterday, Glenn was quiet.

This morning I woke up under the weather and texted them that I wouldn't be going in. None of them responded and yet I watched their vehicles pull out of the gravel drive at their usual time. Since none of them had come looking for me, I figured they got the message.

Assholes.

I wipe my temples with my wrist, the cool rag on my head making my hair damp. Frustratingly enough, they are the assholes I want. Turning on my side, letting my fever paint beautiful dreams behind my eyes, I doze off.

Darkness drifts over my eyelids, and in mere seconds, I jolt awake. Standing over me is Glenn, his suit coat hooked by a finger over his shoulder, a look of concern carved into his stern features.

"What are you doing at home?" I ask groggily, tipping up and glancing at my cell phone screen from beside me. "It's not even lunch time yet."

"Making sure you're okay," he says, eyes never leaving mine. My thighs flex together as my pussy flutters. I can smell his cologne from here, the hair on the back of my neck rising with a tingle in response.

"I'm fine." My body starts slow, rolling shudders as my teeth begin to chatter.

Glenn casts his suit jacket along the foot of the bed, dipping down to grab me up. Pushing against his chest, my cool compress falls to the floor with a saturated thud.

"What are you doing?" I protest, but the truth is, I really just don't want him this up close while I look like shit. His pecs are solid, his core tight against the meaty part of my thigh.

"Helping you."

I roll my eyes as he walks us toward the ensuite bathroom. "You're a few years too late," I mutter, adoring his chest and arms, keeping me safe, no matter what bratty thing I say.

Stopping in his tracks, Glenn presses his lips to my ear.

"I wouldn't change anything."

My mind plays his words on an unending loop as he closes the distance to the bathroom, sitting me carefully on the closed toilet seat.

He wouldn't change how he didn't take an active role in my life until a few weeks ago? He would let me go neglected all over again?

Okay, maybe I wasn't *neglected* because Mari was everything. But... ignore me that intensely *all over again*?

He rolls up his sleeves, starts the bathtub, and plugs the drain.

"Stand."

I do.

"Arms up."

Up go my arms.

Our gazes collide, the air around us stifling with pain and pleasure. In one quick movement, my shirt is over my head, off and tossed to the ground.

Leaving me in *only* panties.

Hooking his thumbs in the filigree lace band, he sinks to the floor, bringing my panties with him. He taps my ankle and I step out, repeating on my other leg.

When he rises, his hardened crotch grazes my hip, and my lips tingle, aching to seal around him.

He outstretches his hand for me to take. Sinking down, the warm water soothes my aching bones and chattering teeth.

I study the outline of his features as he fiddles with the hot and cold dials on the wall. "Are you going to look at me?" I ask, knowing he wants to. Because I've felt the crotch of his Italian slacks against me. There's a mouth-watering bulge.

He gives himself permission to roam below the surface of the water, taking in my body not for the first time. Still, he licks his lips like a starved man.

"We need to talk," I whisper, my eyes dropping to the erection between his legs.

"When you're well, we will." His eyes hover on my labia as he adjusts the collar of his shirt with a groan.

Steam clouds my vision. Maybe the privacy of the bathroom with the walls protecting us from any noise or distraction is what fogs my mind. Whatever it is, I feel bold enough to take what I want.

"Will you stay here with me?"

He nods, eyes circling one pert nipple peeking through the surface. "Yes."

"Sit next to the tub?" I nod to the stool with rolled towels on top. He repositions the towels on the counter and lowers his large frame onto the stool, the seat just slightly below the edge of the tub.

"Will you lower your pants?"

My breath hiccups on the question. Why my confidence has evaporated, too, I'm not sure. Beneath the surface, my body is wracked with nerves. What if he says no? The things that have been happening lately are bold, life-changing things, but all at *their* hands.

This moment is for *me* to have power, and if he really wants me the way he's proclaimed, nothing will stop him from giving it to me.

His eyes hold mine, full of deep-rooted intrigue. "What did you ask me to do?"

I swallow, sinking a bit deeper into the tub, my mouth barely above the surface.

"Lower your pants."

He looks like he's going to ask a question but immediately snaps his mouth closed. With his eyes intensely focused on mine, he brings his hands to his belt and goes to work. Lifting off the stool enough to lower them, Glenn slides his slacks and boxer briefs to just above his knees before settling back down. The tail of his shirt covers his cock, but the nubbed swollen sac between his legs is visible. And mouth-watering.

I stare at them, maybe too long, I don't know. They are *balls*, nothing I've ever been fond of before. But Glenn's are large and plump, and imaging the rest of him sends an achy thrill through me.

"Move your shirt," I say a little breathlessly with how eager I am for the big reveal. My eyes go to his. He wears a miniscule smirk on his lips that I can't ignore, cock reveal or not.

"What?" I bite my bottom lip.

"Have you thought about this before?" he asks, suddenly stripped of his ego, a raw vulnerability left simmering in its wake.

Still biting my bottom lip, I nod.

There were a few despicable times in my hungry youth where I ached endlessly for something confusingly undefined. Glenn and his sons are handsome, and there's something about anger that clouds our logical thought, rendering us completely malleable to the world around us.

That's what I'm saying happened to me those times I touched myself in my bedroom, eyes held shut tightly to allow a backdrop to my fantasies. Glenn and I in bed together, his arms holding me with tender delicacy, in a way I've never craved. Not at all. But he held me like he was protecting me from the world. His cock would throb against my thigh as I would drag my tongue across the prodigious arch of his hardened pectorals.

That's all it would take. I would never even make it to the part where I'd find out what his fingers felt like spreading me apart. The imaginary feel of him against me was enough to send me over the edge, more than a few times.

I hated myself post-coital.

How could I want that from such a cold, unloving, and potentially dangerous man?

Admitting I wanted anything of the kind made me disgusted with myself.

Now I know more about love, not because I'm aged and

wise, but because I've lived through heartache and hell. Pain sears lessons into you about love far more easily than years.

Life and love are one; that's what I've learned.

Neither are easy; they're both dependent upon each other, neither able to fully function alone, not without its mate.

And another thing I've learned about life and love is that it's never going to be just what you expect. There will be a wrench in the plan. A rainy day. An unexpected hiccup.

The point is, things happen. I know after living in misery for most of my youth that happiness is a choice. Poisoning your own life because your dreams didn't come true is a choice that only hurts yourself.

I'm done being my own poison.

These men have been a part of me forever. Whether we were all broken together, unable to really love—because I realize I wasn't a peach when contact was initiated. Not saying it wasn't warranted because it was, but still, I can see things clearly. Pain forces you eventually to wake up.

I woke up when I was eight, when I stopped trying to be loved and hardened myself.

And it's happening again now. Only now, I'm letting myself be loved and dropping the wall from around me.

I remember my mom's laugh. The veracity of her smile when she was with Glenn. A man like that is a good man. My good man, one that my mother would approve of and love.

His sons are no different, part of him, the man my mother loved heart and soul. I've read her diaries; I remember the way she gripped his shirt as they hugged in the kitchen over a pot of warm milk. They were making Nesquik for me before bed. Mom said no, Glenn said yes. She giggled as his hands ran up her nightshirt. He pushed his body against hers, and her back went to the fridge, knocking a magnet to the floor. She laughed, her cheeks were pink, and he whispered to her. And I remember I was smiling, too.

I may not get the answers I need at this moment, but I will get them. I know it. I can't begin to think about what I'll do with them.

"How often did you think about it?" he asks, voice smoky and hoarse, bringing me back to the present. It makes my breasts ache, my nipples tender.

"Plenty."

He nods, giving a small grunt of acknowledgment as his fist knocks the shirt back, exposing his cock as he pumps it.

It's thick, making the corners of my jaw heat in anticipation. He's thicker than his sons, the slick reddened cap of his head wider, too. My eyes fall back to those tremendous balls, the pebbled skin darkening as he thickens in his own palm. The ragged skin of his palm grazing the hot slick flesh of his cock is all I can hear as he touches himself. My body goes to flames in the lukewarm water, every muscle below my hips cinching tight. Tightening his grip on his head, he chokes his fist down his length, exposing the glistening head of his cock to me again.

My tongue clings to the roof of my mouth, dry and thirsty. So fucking thirsty.

"Is this what you want from me, Cherry?" His words sweep through my belly, leaving my pulse broken. Between my thighs, embers turn to small flames as he smooths the pad of his thumb along his vast slit.

I nod, my mouth dipping below the surface. Startling myself I cough, and with my eyes back on him, I find him smiling.

But still stroking.

Warmth gushes from me, spreading down the split of my thighs. Glenn reaches out, plunging his arm into the tub between my feet. He pulls the drain slightly, and the water begins a slow pull-down.

Arm still moving, he uses his other arm to brace himself on the tub, leaning over me. Our eyes hold for a moment but the spell is broken when he breaks the surface of the water, dipping his face in. In the warmth, his mouth seals to my breast. He sucks me hard, sliding his mouth over my flesh until he reaches my nipple. His groan melts into me as he tongues the stiff peak of my sensitive nipple.

The water reveals his nose and allows him a breath, which he takes gracefully. No surprise that this man is a graceful lover. Seeing him sexy like this; hard for me–it's fucking surreal. Every part of me, the insecure, the unsure, the tired, the angry–every version of me wants to experience being the object of a man's affection–especially the Mason men.

He sucks my nipple into his mouth, this time biting down gently. Teeth pinching my nipple, his tongue swipes my areola as his groan vibrates through my chest, making me go a little crazy. I need him so bad.

His lips tickle my wet nipple as he speaks. "I want to fuck you, Cherry, I'm not gonna pretend that I don't." His arm pumps a bit faster, and the spot between my legs nearly catches on fire in full.

"But we're all there or we don't do it."

My veins incinerate as my cunt pulses in waves of desperate hunger. He and his sons want to have sex with me all at once, and it's special enough to them to have a secret code of fucking ethics to abide by? *Don't do her alone, we do her together?*

It should turn my stomach and pour ice water on the flames engulfing my heart, but it doesn't.

It doesn't *at all.*

"Come for me, Glenn," I say, bargaining. Because I want more than nothing, that's for fucking sure.

"Sit up," he says, reaching in again to drain the rest of the water.

The water bubbles a moment and begins its descent as I align my mouth with Glenn's groin, positioning my knees against the porcelain tub.

Eagerly, I lean in, my tongue curling to accommodate the drool in my mouth at the sight of his cock bared to me. But he pulls back, taking the side of my face in his palm. His fingers feel rough against my soft skin, and the contrast sets off a ripple of goosebumps all over my body.

"*I'm* coming *for you*. You're not making me come."

I don't know what he means but I don't want to ask. Asking means talking. "Then do it," I respond boldly, sticking my damp chest out toward him, nipples pebbled.

"I want you to come all over my tits. No one's ever done that to me before," I admit, breathing heavily, a weighty pulse between my thighs keeping me grounded to my spot.

A few strands of dark hair fall free as his head tips forward, hand pumping much faster now. He bats the hair back, giving me a look at the strain in his face. His brow pinched, jaw set.

"Come for me," I say again, feeling emboldened by his unraveling. And so soon, too. I feel suddenly heady with power. "Come now, Glenn."

Jerking his head up, he looks at me before squeezing his eyes shut. Pumping himself slowly, he twists his head, sliding down to the base. Holding his thick erection out like a loaded weapon, he grips it painfully, eyelids fluttering.

The first spurt of come sprays my collarbone and neck. The next straight at my chest, rolling down my cleavage, coating my nipples. He aims and he douses me, hot come nearly coating my entire chest. Or at least it feels that way.

Breathless, he stands there holding his dripping, pulsing cock, his head back.

"Remember what you were doing before that? When there was water in the tub?"

Dropping forward, his gaze locks to mine. "Yes." His dark eyes go to my come covered nipples, then back to me. His lips twitch, and my stomach flutters.

"Do it again. Now."

He drops to his knees, porcelain keeping us apart. And when he seals his lips to my breast, tasting his own release, my knees draw to my chest. I can't help it.

"Touch me," I whimper. *An actual whimper*, because holy shit, he did it. He licks his lips and bites into my neck, sucking my skin as his fingers drive between my lips, stroking my swollen clit.

He tastes my neck, moaning private admissions of desire, coaxing me to lose control for him. Thick fingers sweep through me, my core spasms as my vision chokes down to a fine point.

"There you go," he groans, his voice getting lost in my damp hair. He rubs me harder as I come in hot, fast waves, my body spasming in the tub. His fingers are electric.

He gives me a minute before helping me out. I may be sated but I still need things from him he hasn't given me yet.

I need answers.

"Glenn, we need to talk."

Eight

"At first, I was only motivated by pain." He strokes a hand down his face and neck, eyes unfocused and lost in thought. "I thought it wouldn't last more than a couple of months. I thought as time went by, I'd be able to look at you and see more than what I'd lost."

"You didn't feel bad for me that I lost my mother and the only other adult that I ever had? You could have given me so much more. Even if it was just five words a day, a hug, one fucking trip to the park. You shut me out."

"I know it's hard for you to understand, Cherry, but... I just, I couldn't move past my pain. I never intended Mari to be a forever thing. I thought she'd help out and get us through the first few months." He leans back, finally meeting my eyes. In earnest, his face is wrecked with his own honesty, and I've never felt closer to him than I do now. And yet, I've never been angrier, either.

"And when did the plan change? When did Mari become... forever?"

His smile is sad. "She was never forever. But things hadn't

gotten better in those first two years and... she made it so much easier for me to detach. When you turned seven, I knew I needed her until you were eighteen. For your sake as much as mine. She brought you happiness and I just... I couldn't."

His truth is painful, but it unlocks me from so many things, too.

"Why did she need to go away? Because you're ready to be the person you couldn't be?" It comes out bratty and I mean it bratty. But for the first time, I don't *want* to mean it that way. My heart and brain have different agendas.

Despite my greatest wants, all of me softens with every one of his admissions.

"She was paid a great deal of money to stay as long as she did. Once we reevaluated all those years ago, we agreed steadfastly on eighteen."

"So she left because it was the end of her contract? And that's why you suddenly care where I go and who I go out with? Because I'm now an obligation you can no longer hire out or avoid?"

"You're so angry, Cherry," he says, and he's right, I am and I have every right to be. But the way his voice breaks, how each syllable is filled with anguish–I'm very quickly losing my fight.

I've been fighting for so long.

To be seen.

To understand *why*.

And while they can never make up for what I've lost, and never undo the past, I am so tired of fighting, so tired of aching to be loved.

Even so, I fold my arms over my chest and remain silent.

"I have cared about you since the day I met you. When I dropped to my knees and pulled you into my arms, since that day, I've loved you, Cherry."

I forbid my eyes to get wet and warm, so I lift my chin. "You have a funny way of showing your love."

And then, like he did when I was four with stringy pigtails and denim overalls, he drops down to his knees at my feet.

"What started as self-preservation to navigate my pain turned into your preservation, baby... I kept Mari and the distance between us because you seemed to be doing so well. I felt selfish sending her back to France when you just started thriving." He shook his head as if his own words and actions over the years confused even himself. "I thought, finally, you weren't broken, so I shouldn't try to fix anything."

He reaches up and fits one of my hands between his two. Warm and solid, the comfort his touch brings is sickeningly powerful.

"I've always wanted you; even with as much as I loved Mari, I wanted you," I admit, staring at his large hands and the sparse dark hair on his knuckles.

"After your mom died, I spent years just trying to survive. After I climbed out of my pain and surfaced, I realized that I'd let you become a stranger to me. I thought the boys and I being in your life would cause you more harm, that our pain would infect you... And then at a certain point I realized I was just lying to myself because I'd really begun to feel different." He swallows and my eyes find him, his face uneasy as he crumbles before me.

"How?"

"You know how. I'm on my knees for you, Cherry. *You know how.*"

My entire body incinerates from the subtext. This is what happens to you when you've been emotionally neglected. He comes on you and licks it off, and you still need to hear the words. "When?"

He lowers his head, collecting a breath to gather his thoughts, presumably. When his eyes find mine again, he's *all* confidence. His sureness makes my stomach flip.

"Since your seventeenth birthday. I came downstairs to find you and Mari making waffles with little pink and yellow sprinkles in them. Do you remember?"

I nod. I can almost smell the vanilla and sugar when I think back to that morning. It was warm, the kind of weather that made a tank top with jeans just perfect. Mari and I had our hair up. The marigolds were blooming in the garden the kitchen overlooked.

He shakes his head, but now a small smile lifts his lips. "From that morning on, I knew the distance I was putting between us was no longer an option. Until you turned eighteen, it was a legal necessity."

The brat in me rears her head. "That's pretty presumptuous of you. Just because you wanted to fuck my brains out doesn't mean I'd have let you, *Glenn*."

His hands grow tight around mine, face turning dark with erotic foreboding. "I had to continue on the way things had been."

"Continue treating me like I don't exist after *years* because what's one more?" My heart is racing from his admission, the wet spot between my thighs pulsing, but I yank my hand away nonetheless. Because what I'm saying is true, and no amount of sexual attraction or deep emotional admissions will change that.

I need more than a skirted-around attempt at an apology–selfish one, at that.

"Get up, because you look like a fool down there."

"I need you to understand that I'm willing to spend the rest of my years making up for lost time." Bravely, he wraps his palms around my thighs, letting his hands slide slowly down my legs.

My body wants to give into him, despite the fact that my brain isn't ready. Because the truth is, his attention fuels me in despicable, shameful ways. Ways that somehow allow me to let go of the past as long as I'm promised a fulfilled future.

But there are two glaring questions that I need answered. I lick my lips and summon the rest of my courage.

"What happened to Max and Conrad's mother, Glenn?"

A double widower.

He *is* a double widower, I remind myself.

Not to mention, he said had he not met my mother, she'd still be here. I know he didn't kill her himself because I was there the morning she died. But... it doesn't mean he couldn't be responsible. I don't understand why he'd do that, but complicated situations deciphered and remembered by children don't always speak the truth.

"She was killed, Cherry." He stays kneeling, his hands sliding up my legs, kneading my inner thighs before smoothing back down to my knees. "Max and Conrad understand your loss, Cherry. They know your pain. The three of you could heal and love one another in a way no one else could."

I blink. "Why are you selling me on them when you're on your knees in front of me?" I think back to being taken by Max and Conrad while Glenn watched. Heat flares inside me, leaving a thin sheen of sweat coating my skin.

He smiles, nothing arrogant or ego-driven, and I hate how much my chest tightens at the sight. Like no matter the answers, I'll be his. Theirs.

"I already told you, we're a package deal."

Just then, Sylvio walks into the kitchen from the butler's pantry, freezing in his steps. "A bad time, Miss Cherry?" he asks, eyes wide yet completely avoiding his rich boss crumbled before me like a starving peasant begging for bread.

I look down to Glenn, his dark eyes still laser focused on me, undisturbed by Sylvio's presence. Not long ago he didn't want me in a robe around Sylvio and now he's begging at my feet for Sylvio to witness and doesn't seem to care at all.

"Stay," I say to Glenn, and he continues rubbing my legs as if Sylvio weren't there at all. Smiling, I repeat the word to the other man in the kitchen.

"Stay, do what you need to do, we're okay, just talking."

Sylvio nods, crouching with a clipboard in front of the wine fridge adjacent to us. He starts scribbling, completely ignoring us. I look back down to Glenn.

"I need to know what happened to Max and Conrad's mother." I swallow down the fear and panic rising in my throat at just the mention of the next part. "And my mother. I need to know what happened. Who killed her."

His dark eyes study mine and all I can think about is how he isn't responding. Any time a man doesn't respond right away, he's crafting his lie. I don't need to be fifty-seven years old to know that; I've met enough men.

"Cherry," he draws my name out like it's gum stuck between his teeth. "I can't give you those answers."

Leaning down, exposing my cleavage to him, I press my lips to his ear. "You three want me? I need answers." I rise and fold my arms over my chest waiting for him to give me what I want because he will.

He *has* to. One more rejection from him...

"I'm sorry, Cherry, I can't."

I press my hand to my lower stomach, clenching it as my heart free falls and crashes there. I'm so mad at myself for being hopeful, for thinking that someone would love me or respect me or find me important enough to know my *own fucking truth*.

"I wanted to believe love and life were just complicated, but that things could work out, despite how fucked up they could get." I shake my head. "You made me a fucking fool." A drop of warm water slides down my cheek.

Glenn Mason is a devil. I should have known better. I step back from him and he tips forward, bracing his weight on his hands in my absence.

"Cherry," he says, only this time it's fast and hungry.

"Glenn." His name twists so unnaturally around my tongue, the metaphor of it too much to think about.

And then, with hot tears of disappointment stinging behind my eyes, I return the favor and turn my back, heading upstairs to my room where I *lock* the door.

Nine

I'm so not in the fucking mood to talk or go through any more emotionally draining bullshit. Seriously, if Glenn expects me to believe he's had some infatuation with me for a year, then I need answers.

If you love someone, you meet their emotional needs.

And I need to know who killed my mother. I need to know what happened to my father, who seemed to disappear from my life around age three, from what I can remember. However, I have no one to ask.

I need to know what happened to Max and Conrad's mom, too, because if Glenn is who I've thought he's been, I can never accept any of him.

The knock comes again, this time louder, and now that I'm really paying attention, it doesn't sound like a knock. The thud comes again and I realize it's the heel of a palm. Well, fuck him, he knows what he needs to do if he wants to really speak with me. He needs to talk first.

And I'm locked and loaded with an earful of *how dare yous* as I hear the door open without my permission. Turning to face him, my first reaction is to shriek as horror buzzes through me.

I am eye-to-eye with a stranger.

A male intruder.

My mind races with a trillion thoughts at once.

If this man is up here, does that mean he killed Glenn? Is Sylvio dead too? Did this man wait in the house earlier, and Glenn and Sylvio are fine? Where are Max and Connie? Why would someone want me? Am I being kidnapped? Is he going to rape me? Will he wear a condom if he rapes me?

Am I going to be killed?

That last thought makes me choke out a sob. "Help!" I scream, and before I can do anything else, he lunges forward and grabs me tight, stifling my mouth with a gloved hand.

"I'm not going to hurt you. I'm not going to hurt you, okay? Just... don't scream or I'll have to knock you out."

My heart hammers in my eardrums. I nod. His arm banding my chest loosens, but his other hand remains on my face. His gloves are fake leather, and they smell and taste like shit.

"I came in the door attached to that room with the little fuckin' bench in it." He lowers his voice as we walk toward my bedroom door. "So that's where we're going. Don't try and make a break for it, sweetheart, or I'll have to drug you, okay?"

He sounds older than Glenn, or maybe Glenn's age. But far less educated than my stepfather, his words running together sloppily. Or maybe he's drunk. Either way, I don't recognize the voice, at all.

"Okay," I say against the glove, and then, because making my captor feel small in any way is definitely stupid but I'm too angry to resist, I add, "it's called the mudroom."

I don't know where Glenn and Sylvio are. If they were still

in the kitchen, I heard nothing. The mudroom is on the opposite side of the house, but even so, the kitchen is mostly open and noise carries easily. Panic flares in my belly, but I tell myself to stay calm because nothing good has ever come from freaking the fuck out.

What feels like years later because my mind is still running a mile a minute, we're outside, the six o'clock sunset is muted in the distance. Where is everyone? Why is this evening the one night that Max, Conrad, and Glenn aren't around? The man shoves me inside a car, but not before taping my mouth and binding my wrists with a zip tie. My nostrils flare as I scream internally at the house in front of me, begging someone, anyone to come outside.

But no one does.

Then the house full of people who pay me no mind begins to grow smaller as the car takes me from the place I've been dying to leave. And yet, I've never wanted to be inside that house with those assholes as much as I do now.

Once the car has gone about a mile from the house, the man driving belatedly speaks, his eyes finding mine in the rearview mirror.

"Don't even recognize me, do you?" he asks, and nothing about him is familiar. Reaching back, he yanks the tape from my face, making me wince. Pain or not, I'm glad to have my mouth back. Breathing and fighting will be much easier now.

"You don't have to pretend we know each other. You already have me in the car. I'm not a six-year-old that needs to be tricked with some phony 'I know you' bullshit." I can't help my sharp words. With my hands behind my back, they are my only weapon.

He chuckles, and though nothing about it is recognizable, the hairs along my neck rise.

My gaze goes to the rectangular mirror, finding him already watching me.

"C'mon, you remember me, don't you, *Cherry*?" he asks, voice still not shaking any cobwebs free.

"Why the fuck did you have to zip tie my wrists? You're a big old man. Are you seriously afraid I'll be able to *fight back*?" The last two words give me the chills because the truth is, this man may be driving me to the last place I'll ever go. I have no clue.

"My step-father is a lawyer, so if you thought you'd swipe some random girl to rape and murder, I hope you're ready for prison because the man lives to fight."

The driver lets loose a laugh, dark and twisted. I don't know how, but I get the feeling I *must* know him because none of this feels random anymore.

"I'm well aware that Glenn Mason likes to fight. The thing is, though, sweetheart, he's not a winner. I've beaten him twice already."

"Yeah?" I ask, surprising myself with such a docile response. But he just confirmed what I'd just figured out–we *aren't* strangers. "And who are you?"

I give up fighting the restraints because it hurts too much, and I'm not magically going to break free. This isn't a movie.

The car ambles down a dirt drive off the main road, the area lush with mature trees and long grass. The perfect place for bad things. Quiet and secluded, yet enough noise from the main road to hide... *screams*.

When he throws the car in park, I want to vomit. Twisting back to face me, his features become hard to ignore. The wide set of his eyes. His *blue* eyes. The same cerulean sea color as *my* eyes.

A photo flashes through my mind. One I found in my

mother's shoe box after she died. Glenn kept the box hidden, but I snatched it one day. It was full of things–but only one photo. It was me as a baby in the arms of... *this* man.

"S-Stan?" I stammer the name. I don't remember him, hardly, but the glare in his eyes matches my own.

"You miss me, Cherry?" he asks, and the way he asks makes me think he genuinely thinks I've been waiting for him to come back.

"How could I miss you? I don't even know you. And I don't know that I ever did."

His smile slithers down my back like an ice cube.

"But you remembered my name, which means you remember me. Somewhere inside, you remember *your old dad*."

My face must fall because he reaches back in an attempt to cup my cheek or some other completely inappropriate shit, but I shirk away.

"Oh come on, Cherry, I'm not the one you should be afraid of." His eyebrows lift. "I'm not the one who hurt your mom."

"Says the kidnapper," I say stupidly, wiggling against the restraints. And then– "Why did you bring up mom and who hurt her?" I don't need thirty years of life under my belt to know guilt when I see it.

"You wouldn't have come with me if I asked nice," he says, his phony charm slipping into a smarmy energy that makes me uncomfortable. "And I only defended myself to you out the gate like that because I know Glenn Mason wants you to believe I had some hand in what happened."

He talks like he's some big bad gangster, his slang nearly Italian at this point. We aren't from Jersey, and he's got blonde hair and blue eyes, just like I do. Everything about him irks me, and suddenly I wish I were at home with Satan and his spawn.

"Glenn Mason has never spoken a word of my mother's murder to me. Not a single syllable," I snark, angry at everyone now that I think about it. I found her, and yet to this day, I don't know any details. An intruder, Mari said, after I pressed her about it once. And that's all she knew. A masked intruder looking to rob the wealthy lawyer, yet Glenn wasn't home when it happened.

Allegedly.

Though I had literally zero details to go on, I spent most of my life believing Glenn was somehow involved. He wasn't there when it happened, after all. Growing up, what I'd learned of crime came from TV and movies; it was usually someone you knew, a family member or friend.

That aligned with Glenn.

The part that I always got hung up on was *why* he'd do it, because the first couple of years after she passed, he was a ghost. He was in pain, and as a child his pain seeped into me with every downtrodden glance and tired sigh.

No one was ever caught, and Glenn was an up-and-coming lawyer, widower once already. No one seemed to point to him, either.

But I'd be no better than the girl in the horror films who locks herself in a bathroom while a murderer is chasing her if I didn't hang onto my suspicion.

Not knowing what role Glenn played made my subconscious desire for his love and attention all those years even more frustrating. I was mad at everyone, including myself.

I still am.

Only now, I have Stan in front of me, and something tells me *he* has answers.

"What do you want with me?" I ask, glancing around me as he unbuckles.

"We're getting out. Then I'll tell you."

When he exits the car, my body floods with nervous energy. Should I try to make a break for it? The road is a half mile behind us, and with my wrists bound I'm not sure I can make it, especially if I fall.

I don't have time to make a hasty plan because Stan is yanking me out and walking me through a grove of Oak trees in an instant. The temperature drops a few degrees the further we go into the woods, and my stomach grows sick.

Father or not, I'm well aware that Stan doesn't give a fuck about me. When I'd ask about my "real" father, Mari told me that he disappeared the year my mother and Glenn married. When I asked her how she knew, she said she asked Glenn that very same question after noticing how detached he was from parenting.

If you love your kid, you don't disappear on them. If they need you, you show up. Easy. He could've come back from wherever he was when mom died. He could've raised me.

But he didn't.

The whoosh of a metal blade makes my heart leap, but my wrists are free. Stan grabs my upper arm and leads me a few more feet until there's a clearing in the trees. Hidden with brush and shrubs is a small–*very fucking small*–cabin.

Somehow, the cabin brings me relief. I was half expecting to walk up to a freshly dug grave.

Once we're inside, he sits me down on a small cot bed and takes a chair across from me. I don't want to but I'm forced to *really* look at him. He's thin and tall, with blonde hair, roots white with age. His skin tells a story of sun exposure and cigarettes, late nights and booze. His fingers are adorned with gold rings, and at the exposed v of his shirt, white chest hair curls. A silk shirt and jeans are his kidnapping outfit of choice, and when I meet his eyes, my lip trembles at how much I look like him and how sick it makes me.

"Why did you take me?" I ask again, confused and really fucking over having the shots of my life called by men that don't even take care of me. *Fuck that.*

"You're eighteen now," he says, dropping his elbows to his knees, leaning forward to find comfort.

I shift, crossing my legs before wrapping myself in my own arms. Eighteen. If he planned all this time just to do something heinous like wait until I was legal to rape me? I'll fight. I'll fight every fucking movement if it comes down to it.

Stan takes notice of my protective shifting and holds up his hands in a truce or surrender. "No, sweetheart. No matter what Glenn has told you, I'm no monster. I'm your father."

"Why did you take me?" I launch the same question at him again.

He glances over his shoulder, like he's making sure we're alone, and I can't help but roll my eyes because he kidnapped and dragged me to a cabin with no windows in the woods. I'm pretty sure no one can hear him.

"Let me guess, Glenn didn't tell you about the money?"

I shake my head, not falling for what clearly feels like a trap. Because explaining legitimate legal issues does not require kidnapping.

"No," I add. "What money?"

A smile quirks his lips but he stifles it, smoothing a hand down his face. God, he's so fucking easy to read. I took the bait, and it literally had him smiling at how easy it was. Idiot.

"Your mom and me, we put away quite a bit of money for you to get your hands on when you turned eighteen. Enough to not just get yourself through school or whatever, but like, new life money," he says, dragging out the last few words to impart importance on me.

"If you and my mom were together happily, why don't I have any memories of you?"

It's not exactly what I want to ask, but I feel unprepared for this moment. Though, to be fair, I don't think I ever dreamed of a time where I came face to face with my sperm donor. It was bad enough to have a stepfather in my daily life that didn't care. I didn't need another uncaring parent, especially a faceless ghost.

He stares at me for a long time, or what feels like a long time. The trees rustle as a breeze makes its way through them. In the distance is a faint whooshing of cars on the country road. Something in the cabin creaks every few seconds.

"You really don't know anything about anything, do you?"

I roll my eyes. "I don't know about *my mother* because she was killed and no one has told me anything about it."

Reaching between his legs, he grabs the chair to scoot closer to me. I don't like that.

"We were happy. Then Glenn Mason came along and stole her. Put ideas in her head that life would be better with him. And he had more money than me, he was fancy," Stan says, staring off into the cabin like he's reliving a specific moment, kept secret from me.

"She had an affair," I state, but even *this* I didn't know about my mom and dad. I really don't know any of their story, or the first chapters of my own, for that matter.

"We were never legally married," he says, "but you were *my daughter*, so that made her mine by default."

I narrow my eyes. "No, that doesn't."

He narrows his back. "You're like her, you know that?"

I tip my chin with defiance. "Unwilling to do what some man says when he stomps his foot like a toddler?"

His eyes narrow for a moment, and his lips twitch. I'm pretty sure an expletive is mumbled, but I don't know for sure because my own rage is simmering loudly over the top of his. "I'm not stomping my foot here, sweetheart. I may tell you some stuff you don't like, but so far the only one acting like a *brat* is you."

"Why am I here?"

He smooths his palms down his legs. "I'm gonna get you your money, then I'll go."

"*If* there is money," I say, knowing there isn't, but still needing to get to the bottom of whatever it is he's up to. "Why are you *helping* me? What's in it for you?"

He leans back, nodding as if he prepared himself for this question. God, he really is so fucking obvious. "I'm leaving the country. I wanted to see my daughter before I left, and leave her with one good deed to remember her pop by."

Isn't all of that *so* fucking convenient.

I don't say anything, so he starts in on what's important.

"So, it's like half a million Glenn's holding for you. He was supposed to give it to you when you turned eighteen, but that rat, I knew he wouldn't."

I cross my legs at the knee and fold my arms over my chest. "And?"

"That's your money, Cherry. Me and your mother didn't put it away for Glenn. It's *yours*."

"If he didn't give it to me by now, what makes you think asking about it is going to do anything? Won't he just lie?"

Stan nods again, prepared for this question, too, it would seem.

"He's all successful and rich now. He don't wanna look like

a bad guy." He leans back again, getting comfortable in his plan. "You say someone's holding you hostage; he'll pay the money."

"So... let me get this straight. This money that's owed to me–*which I've heard nothing about*–is being held by my rich stepfather who is unwilling to give it to me... even though he's rich," I say, and Stan has feedback.

Waving a finger he says, "it's not about money to him. To him it's about winning. He took your mother and the last thing he's taking is that money." He shakes his head, believing his own bullshit I think. "It's all for his big fuckin' ego."

"So," I continue, "I am telling him *I'm kidnapped* in order to get the money rightfully owed to me even though he could have me arrested for this." I scoot to the edge of the bed, uncrossing my legs. "And then I'm supposed to take off randomly after being kidnapped? Just scam him and then... disappear?"

His face falls reactively for a second before he gathers it back up again with a smile and a nod. "Right."

Why did his face fall?

Oh my god. *He's* going to take the money, and I *am* going to disappear.

Fuck.

Ten

He tilts his head to study me. I think he's trying to intimidate me but I refuse to react.

He's probably going to kill me. But I refuse to be scared. I will not give him an ounce of power.

"This is never going to work, you know," I lie with confidence, because at this point, what other option is there? Getting in his head is all I have.

"Why's that?" Stan pulls a toothpick from his breast pocket and slips it between his teeth.

"They won't pay you."

There it is again. Stan's face falls south for a moment, like even though he's a piece of human garbage that cares nothing about lives, *this* got to him. He picks it back up quickly, giving me a simple smile. Another piece of ice seems to slide down my spine.

"They'll *definitely* pay."

I swallow, keeping my eyes trained on him, refusing to let my rapid heartbeat call the shots. I have to stay calm.

"You're going to make me tell them I'm kidnapped and to

drop money somewhere to get me back?" I ask, unimpressed. But he's right, they will do it. I know they will.

"Yes."

"So why are you going to kill me after?"

"Whoa, whoa, whoa. Who said that? I didn't say that."

"Your face said it for you, Stan." Fuck. I was right. Why the fuck did I have to be right and why the hell did I not have my cell phone on me? I'll never be able to call for help, if I even get the chance anyway.

"Listen, Cherry, there's no harm in what we're doing here. Okay? They got the money."

"I thought it was *my* money."

"You know what I mean." He's growing irritable, which isn't great for me, but I can't stop pushing his buttons. If this is it, I'm not going down easy.

"No, actually, I don't. Because we aren't Robin Hoods, okay? You're robbing them and using me as bait. There is harm in this, and I don't think I'm owed any money."

The anger in his eyes dances like blue flames. I press on.

"I get why I had to be eighteen, too. In case you got caught, don't want the charges of abducting a minor."

Stan's face droops in slow motion shock, like he can't possibly comprehend that I've solved him in a matter of minutes.

Then I deliver the truth.

"This won't end well for you."

Nervously, he digs his cell phone out, sending a text message. He types with one finger and minutes pass as I grow more and more panicked. What if they don't come? What if they choose not to bargain or some other moralistic high ground bullshit, calling Stan's bluff?

He'll kill me.

I fucking know it.

"There," he says, resting the phone on top of his thigh. "Now we wait."

"You texted them?"

He nods. "Smart, right?"

I blink. "Cops will just ping you and know exactly where we are so... yeah." I nod. "Very smart."

He smirks knowingly. "This phone goes off Wifi, not GPS. It's an Android. I use a VPN. Can't be tracked."

That was annoyingly unexpected.

"Wow, do you work for Apple?" I roll my eyes, my pulse a stark contrast to what would appear to be a cool, collected persona.

"You are like your mom; you know that?" Stan slinks forward like a raccoon going to trash. "Smart fuckin' mouth."

His phone vibrates, the screen coming alive. He reads the message, as slowly as I'd imagine he reads. *Slow.*

"They're making the drop in fifteen," he smiles at the screen for a long, weird moment before looking up at me.

"Here?" My hopes skyrocket. "So, you're giving me back to them?"

He blinks. He drops to his knees, ducking between my legs to drag something out from beneath the cot. Looking down, he's pulled out a sepia leather bag, quite long in length, with a shoulder strap attached. A zipper traces the bag, and he finds the end easily before tugging it open.

With a whoosh, there is my answer.

A gun. And a big one at that.

Men like him would have to resort to violence–they don't know enough words to communicate. *Me mad, gun good* is about as far as men like Stan have come.

"Don't worry about anything, Cherry, okay? You... it's not gonna be long."

Fuck. Fucking fuck. Now is the time to cry and beg, drop to my knees and plead for my life. Say *no, no, don't do this.*

But neither of us have the chance to do anything but turn our heads and stare, mouths agape. Outside there is a distinct noise. The quick approach of a vehicle followed by the uproarious screech of sudden breaks.

Someone is here.

It can't be them. They're over twenty minutes away, I think, though I can't remember exactly.

I don't know if I should be happy or terrified further, but for some reason, the fact that Stan looks worried gives me fucking hope.

"Stay the fuck here." He says angrily, grabbing the gun from the velvet lined bag. He exits the tiny cabin a moment later.

Car doors, multiple, but I can't really tell how many because my ears are throbbing with an incessantly loud drumming. My pulse, my heart, my small existence bouncing before me too quickly to catch.

Loud voices are cast back and forth from the front of the cabin to a few paces away. Deep enough to rattle through me but just low enough to escape my ears.

Honestly not knowing is worse than knowing. Staying in suspense is doing me no favors. My hand trembles for a moment but I get it in check before pushing open the already cracked door. The setting sunlight streams over my face, too bright for my good. I put a hand up, blinking a few times to regain my sight. After the yellow orb in my peripheral vision fades, the horizon comes into focus, four men standing before me.

Stan.

And *them*.

How did they get here so fast? It's like they left right after I got taken or something. And with the money already?

No.

My eyes go to their hands, and Stan argues with Conrad, but I tune them out. None of them are holding anything. No shady suitcases or duffle bags or whatever the fuck dirty money is exchanged in.

There is no money.

"Where's the fucking money?" Stan asks again, this time raising his gun to Conrad, though his finger isn't over the trigger. Yet.

Still, raising the gun crosses a line. Shows his intentions.

I hate that we share blood.

"I'll ask one more time," Stan goes on, nudging Conrad because they're standing next to one another. Slowly, Max and Glenn come around the hood from the driver's side to cage him in. Stan slinks back a few steps, and in a matter of seconds, the man with the gun becomes powerless. Max's hand curls around the barrel, and one jerk has the gun out of Stan's possession.

If I weren't slightly terrified and hugely confused, maybe I'd even laugh at how weak and pathetic the man who lent me DNA is.

Glenn looks me up and down. "Cherry, are you okay?"

I nod.

"Tell me what happened," he says, his voice full of calm determination.

Stan lunges for Conrad; why, I have no idea because all three of the Mason men are twice the build as my father. For some reason, though, he believes he's going to get away from this hostage situation *he* created.

Conrad grabs Stan by the throat, letting punches connect with his chest with seemingly no impact. Holding Stan at a distance, he looks at Max for an answer. Turning to his father, gun not pointed at anyone, Max asks, "what do you want me to do with him?"

"I want to hear from Cherry what happened," Glenn says slowly, returning his focus to Stan. "Can you keep your mouth shut long enough for her to speak?"

Max raises the long end of the gun and taps Stan's hand, which makes him visibly uncomfortable. "I can give you an incentive to stay quiet. Like, I'll blow your hand off if you don't."

Stan's face drains of color as he nods, Max using the gun to lead us back inside the small, makeshift cabin. Once inside, Glenn and Conrad sit on either side of me on the cot; Max holds the gun at Stan as Stan practically melts to the floor, slouched against the wall.

Ten minutes ago, he was a technical genius and now he looks like he's one scary threat away from pissing himself. Fucking pathetic.

The Mason men came and took control of this in minutes.

They're saving me.

"Cherry," Glenn puts his hand on my knee, eliciting a disgruntled noise from Stan's throat. Max prods him with the gun and he traps the noise, shutting up for his own good.

"Tell us what happened, okay, beautiful?"

I recount the details of my abduction, leaving nothing out. I tell them how Stan said he and my mother put money away and that he's helping me get it. The entire time, Stan's head hangs low, telling me what a crock of shit all of it was.

"You wanted answers, and I'll tell you right now, the reason I didn't want to give you the answers you wanted is because of this man, right here." He motions to Stan, who still doesn't lift his head.

"Even though he's a fucking waste of life, he is the man who gave you life. At least partially. And I wanted you to have the option to know him, if you wanted."

"How does that have anything to do with what happened to my mother? Or Conrad and Max's mother? Because those were the questions I wanted answers to. I never asked about Stan"

Conrad's hand comes down on my thigh, solid and reassuring, helping me to stay grounded during this tornado of information. I put my hand on top of his, and I notice that Max and Glenn notice, too.

"Your father killed our mother, Cherry. Then he killed yours, too." Conrad's words are so quiet and soft, like wrapping a dagger in velvet will change the outcome.

"What?" I ask, confused. This entire time I've lived my life believing Glenn had something to do with it all, somehow, someway.

I can't deny the relief coursing through me knowing that the man I've grown attracted to, that I've painfully yearned after for years is... innocent. With this new information, I spend a few seconds reframing moments of my life where I felt disgusting and wrong.

"Candy and I fell in love. It was an attraction that neither of us could deny. We tried to stop it. I was married. She was *with* your father. Adulterers were not who we wanted to be," Glenn says carefully, keeping his eyes on mine. Conrad's fingers curl deeper into my thigh.

"I told my wife that I had fallen for someone else. She was... heartbroken. But she didn't hate me. Max and Conrad can attest to this. Lola never hated me. She understood that love is the human condition and that we're destined to chase it wherever it takes us."

Max speaks up, still keeping Stan silent by holding the gun to his back. "It's true. When Dad was moving out, she said that this was the right thing for our family because two happy families in separate homes are better than one home full of unhappy people."

"She was happy? She met someone too?" I ask, feeling so bad for this dead woman who gave birth to these two beautiful men.

Glenn shakes his head. "She had the dream of moving on, but she was still mending her heart."

"She didn't harbor hatred because Dad was honest with her." Conrad is still so gentle when he speaks, even though this is his trauma now, too.

Glenn nods. "I was."

I stare at Stan's head, moving slightly now like he wants to argue against this but doesn't have the courage.

"What happened?" I quietly ask.

Glenn begins speaking but I shake my head. "I want to hear it from Stan."

Finally, we're eye to eye again. His face is impassive, like none of this no longer holds any emotional value to him.

"She was coming out of the grocery store. I asked her out, but she knew who I was. Knew I was Candy's man. She told me to let it go. She said we weren't allies unless my cause was also moving on."

Conrad's knee begins to bounce, so I shift our linked hands to his leg, soothing him.

"What did you do?" Glenn asks. "Tell her what you did, Stan."

"I shot her. Because if I couldn't have my wife, I didn't want him to have his."

"She had nothing to do with it," Max says, his voice surprisingly raw. It's been years but you never get over the loss of a parent. That much I understand.

"That's when you and your mom came to live with me and the boys. The boys needed another adult. I was overwhelmed. And your mother and I still planned to be together, despite the tragedy."

Stan laughs. "I even let you marry her."

Glenn stares into Stan's eyes as he relives his painful past. "We thought you were on the run after killing Lola. We got married thinking that despite the tragic start, we'd be able to have the life we dreamed of."

"What happened to my mom?" I can't help but ask again because even though I know the answer, I just don't know why. "You shot her, too?" I ask, directing the question just to Stan.

"If you couldn't have her, neither could I. Isn't that right? Didn't matter you were taking yet another mother from her children, just so long as you got your anger out, right?"

Stan smooths his tongue across his teeth, and my skin crawls in response. "The world is a better place without two cheating whores."

Glenn ignores the ugly words pouring from my father's mouth and turns to me. "I didn't want to tell you your father had killed them, I thought you wouldn't believe me. I thought you'd only hate me more for exposing the truth." I need to process that and not in front of four men.

I look at Max because I'm still holding unanswered questions. "How did you guys get here so fast?"

Conrad takes over. "I went up to check on you after I came home, and Dad said you guys argued. You were gone, and it had only been a few minutes, so we came for you."

"How did you know where to find me if you didn't get the phone call with the location until just ten minutes ago?"

The three Mason men share a glance.

"What?"

"We've had a tracking device on you for a while, Cherry. We were afraid Stan might resurface."

"For money?" I ask, facing Stan once more.

Glenn nods. "We put tracking devices in the soles of your shoes and a few other places, Cherry." He gives a despondent smile. "I'm sorry. I realize it's a violation of your privacy–"

"It saved your life," Max interjects.

"And it let *you* know every date I ever went on," I add, looking at Conrad, who admitted he knew I've been on forty-six dates.

He shrugs. "The trackers helped but it was that *and* good old fashioned stalking."

"So let me get this straight. You guys have been lying to me about my mother's death, about my father's life, about.... *Everything*."

Glenn accepts responsibility. "Yes."

"But for your good," Conrad adds.

The three of them tense, like warriors preparing for the gates to open, ready to do battle with me.

Except they're reading me wrong.

I'm not angry.

I've been angry too long.

I know we can't just leap into perfection and put the past behind us entirely, but we can give up our anger and take a step forward. After dog paddling in emotional chaos for years, it feels like we really can truly move forward.

Once I know they are *truly* devoted to me.

"Cherry, say something." Glenn tries to disguise the worry in his tone, but it's there, rattling around his chest. He drags the heel of his palm down his sternum, soothing his worries.

I face Stan, and my lip trembles meeting the pair of eyes that so closely resemble mine.

"You killed two mothers."

He rolls his eyes. "You're fine, Cherry. You got money and these motherfuckers. Don't play the victim. You're too old. It's not flattering."

I blink. My brain struggles to calibrate that this man is part of me. A man so stupid and morally devoid. My eyes rise to Max.

Max pumps the shotgun, sending an empty cartridge to the floor. I wonder if that cartridge was from when Stan shot my mom.

"Cherry, wait outside," Glenn instructs and he and Conrad get to their feet.

They don't want me to see this, and truthfully, I don't want to see it either. When I'm stepping out into the sun, a blast rattles through me, making my ears pound and my bones shake.

My breath catches, and a moment later, the three of them emerge. With my back to Glenn's SUV, I take in the sight. I don't know who pulled the trigger. One of them did. All of them did, in a way. And now, we're in this together.

"Give us five minutes, then we're going home."

I nod, though my eyes can't sit still as they roam up and down the long, tanned arms of both of my step-brothers, searching for blood. Then I see Glenn's neck. A spray of crimson. A few blots over his chest. The toes of his shoes are sticky with the thick, dark liquid, dirt clinging to the blood.

"You're ours now, Cherry." Max's voice is unwavering. My nipples stiffen.

"Say it," Glenn says, his voice growing desperate and quick, like he's starved and ready to tear into his meal. His pink tongue drags over his bottom lip, dark hair falling across his forehead. "Say it."

"Tell Dad you're ours," Conrad coaxes, always the gentle voice of reason.

"I'm yours," I say, dizzy from the way those two words make so much sense.

Max's eyes glaze with heat. "Prove it to us."

My chest hollows with an anticipatory dizzying exhale. I notice just then, my hands begin to tremble. My bottom lip, too. I didn't love Stan. Fuck, I barely even knew Stan. But I cannot ignore the sickness churning in my belly as I stare into the crimson splash of blood across Glenn's chest.

"Get her in the car," Glenn says. And from there, things get kind of blurry.

Max makes a private phone call, and I watch through the windshield from the backseat as Glenn and Conrad strip down to nothing, stepping into clothes from a canvas bag they'd pulled from the car. Max does the same when he's off the phone.

Glenn drives the SUV, Max and Conrad sandwich me in the backseat. I can't calm, despite the fact that I now have the answers I told myself were the last thing keeping me from them. I can't clear my head. My nerves race so loudly I can hardly hear anything but my own freaked-out breath.

Conrad cradles the back of my neck in his large palm,

kneading away my stress. Max takes my hand with his, waffling our fingers together before resting them on his lap.

No sooner is the door shut and locked at home does Glenn have my hair tangled between his knuckles, my head yanked back. Standing over me, he aligns his mouth above mine and whispers to me.

"I failed you then, but I'll never fail you again."

Belts whoosh, zippers descend, a pile of clothes grows on the floor as Glenn's mouth comes down over mine, hot and needy.

His tongue twists around mine, his mouth warm and sweet. The back of my head burns where he tugs but it sends a spark down my spine, igniting my lower half.

Our kiss breaks when Conrad and Max position themselves on either side of me, completely bare. Their long, solid fingers slide beneath the fabric of my dress straps, tugging them down. A hand pulls the zipper at my back, but my head is growing so fuzzy from the heat between us all that I'm not sure who it is.

When a rush of cool air hits me, I look down to see my dress pooled at my ankles, Conrad and Max working my thong down my hips, too.

Max sinks his lips into the side of my neck as Glenn's hand reaches between my legs. I jump a little–even though I want it–my body is still reeling from what just happened in the woods.

They killed *someone* bad... for me.

Conrad sucks my earlobe into his mouth, nibbling gently as he reaches up to cup my breast closest to Max.

"Dad wants you first." His lips move to the stiff peak of my breast, still gripping the other one tightly. Before he seals his mouth to my nipple, he says, "let Dad make you feel good."

That's when the full body trembles take over. Head to toe, I shake uncontrollably like I'm attempting Everest in shorts and a tank. Glenn's hand slides between my thighs, the tip of his thumb sweeping between my labia in a whisper of a touch. I want to give in to the heat inside of me, embrace the erratic heartbeat and overwhelming desire to be devoured whole by the three of them.

But the trembling keeps me stuck, my body rigid between the three of them. Glenn brings his mouth down over mine as Conrad sucks my breast, holding the other one for Max to suck too. He does, and before I give my lips to Glenn, I look to see Max drag his tongue over Conrad's grip on my breast before he too begins to suck the peak.

"What's going to happen?" I whisper, voice earthquake levels of a tremble as I try desperately not to cry. Suddenly I'm overcome with panic and fear, and that's the *only* reason tears are sneaking up on me. "To you guys?" I finish right before Glenn swallows my words with his powerful mouth.

The way his tongue pulls me closer is something I've never experienced, and it makes me even wetter. And he knows it. His thumb, still playing between my lips, torques around my clit, making tight, pressure-filled circles, driving me insane. My head falls back, and it's that opening that Max and Conrad take to bring their mouths to my exposed nape, peppering sloppy kisses all over my skin.

"It's taken care of," Glenn answers. And as if he's putting to rest worries that I don't even know I'm going to have, he adds, "no one's ever going to know the four of us were there."

"Listen to Dad, Cherry," Max groans, his mouth now pressed behind my ear. Conrad's palm moves around my breast as he still enjoys the column of my throat, no doubt leaving marks from how passionate he kisses and sucks.

My body trembles nonetheless, and I know it will take more than a few verbal assurances to calm me down.

The wide pad of Glenn's thumb stops directly over my swollen clit. Moving it slowly back and forth, he tugs my head back again, making sure my eyes are on him when he speaks.

"Listen to your brothers." He kisses me again, stealing away my breath, letting my mind wander from the vibrating bang in that cabin, just for a second. "Everything is finally as it should be."

"They're not..." I pant, unable to finish my sentence as Glenn falls to a crouch in front of me, nuzzling into my cunt with the bridge of his nose, making me whine. "My brothers...." the last two words tumble from my lips but never seem to crash to the floor.

The four of us being together awakened a cyclone of rampant thoughts and fears inside me, making me twist under Glenn's hold, physically unable to sit still with the chaos storming inside me.

"Everything is finally as it should be," Glenn repeats before sealing his lips over my clit, severing all ties from what had happened earlier. The trembling rolls to a halt as my spine starts to waver for reasons completely unrelated to that boom in the cabin.

"Yes," I moan, a jolt of pain surging through my breast where Conrad nipped with more force. Max takes my hand from Glenn's shoulder—I didn't even know it was there—and fills it with his straining, impressive cock. Between the tongue bowering my most sensitive bit, the mouth paying my nipple more attention than anyone ever had, and the hardened cock in my palm... my utter unraveling is underway.

"Come for Dad," Conrad rasps, releasing my breast with a wet pop of his lips. He kisses me, feeding his fingers through the side of my hair, taking my attention completely. Our tongues twist together as his cock presses against my side. He paints my hip with a smear of liquid, and I moan in response to how they both leak for me. My hand idly pumping Max is getting wet, too.

Thumbs drive into the meaty part of my thighs, forcing me to step apart, taking my lips from Conrad, forcing me to look down. Glenn nuzzles deeper into me as a thread of precome connects the swollen crown of his cock to the mud room floor below.

Holy fuck. Three men are weeping to fuck me.

Abandoning my fears that the world wouldn't understand, that we were doing something wrong, I lean into all the fucking amazing things I'm finally feeling, not just between my legs but beneath my ribs, too.

My heart seems to have grown, beating strong and proud in my chest.

Glenn was right.

My personal Satan and his spawn are putting my world on its head in the best way possible. Very quickly, they are becoming... *my everything.*

Two solid fingers drive up inside me, making me jump. Max and Conrad keep me in place as Conrad slips his cock into my other hand. I pump them both, letting my head fall back as they sink their mouths into my neck like hungry vampires. Glenn furls his fingers inside me, the tips connecting with that secret, warm spot inside me.

His tongue flicks against my clit, back and forth, as he pumps and curls his fingers in a blindingly hot pattern.

"I'm... I'm..."

"Come," Max rasps desperately in my ear, both he and his brother now sucking on the ends of my lobes, teasing me. I pump them harder as Glenn sends me over the edge, growling into my cunt as I start to spasm. My eyes close, despite having a beautiful erotic movie in front of me in the form of my Mason men.

But I can't help it. It all feels... too good.

"*Coming...*" I finish my sentence, even though I've been spasming around Glenn's digits for a few seconds already. He moans, his lips and stubble sending a vibration through my hip bones as he eats me through my entire orgasm.

I run my thumbs over the cocks in my palms, warming from the slick arousal.

Before I can even tip my head forward and thank the man between my thighs for the mind-blowing orgasm, he hoists me over his shoulder, my entire lower half naked and glistening from the orgasm.

I should scream to be put down; I should feel nervous about being put on such a vulnerable display for Max and Conrad. But when they begin kissing the backs of my thighs, my core releases stress and I melt into Glenn's body.

Without a word, Glenn makes his way upstairs. I can see Max and Conrad's shadows on the wall behind us as they follow us up. We end up in Glenn's room—one I haven't seen since I was a child. Glenn handles me like a doll, lifting me by the hips to set me down. I'm placed on the bed, in the center.

Max climbs on, lying on his back next to me, weaving our fingers together in an intimate way I didn't expect from him.

But then, they are giving everything to me, because that's what we are now. We're everything which means doing stuff outside your comfort zone.

I know I have to do the same for them.

"Are you ready?" Conrad asks. Glenn is passing his son a bottle of lube, palming his shiny erection. Conrad squirts some into his palm and begins stroking himself too. The sound of alpha palms strangling dominant cocks makes my mouth water. My legs spread, and when my mind catches up, I approve.

I don't know how I'll take them all, but I will.

"Yes."

Glenn knees his way onto the bed, his cock resting in his palm. I've seen him before, but I can't help but stare in awe like it's the first time. I notice things now more than I did in the bathroom earlier. He's thick, I remember that, and I'd expect no less with a man as powerful as him. There's a slight curve in his cock, and I can't help but wonder if that will work to my benefit, making him hit my spot right away. Below his thick, long shaft are two of the biggest balls I've laid eyes on. They look bigger now than before, or maybe I'm just hungrier.

A shade darker than the glistening russet color of his cock, they're full, drooping heavily between his spread thighs. Catching me eyeing them, he lets a grin curl his lips. "They need to be drained. Can you drain them, Cherry?"

Holy shit. I take a few extra breaths in response to his filthy words. I nod, and I feel Conrad knee his way onto the bed next to me.

Max puts his cock in my hand and begins pushing his hips toward me, moaning dirty words just like his dad. "You'll be so good at taking the three of us, Cherry. I know it." He sucks my fingers into his mouth, and that's when Conrad steals my attention.

Letting his cock bob above my face, still on his knees over me, Conrad grips my chin with more force than I thought he was capable of. "Face me," he whispers, a sweet smile on his lips as he tenderly strokes my blonde hair, yet I know we aren't on the cusp of a tender moment.

I love that Conrad is a *teddy bear* with a streak of dirty dom somewhere inside of him, a part of him that only rears its head in response to how he feels for *me*. I bring out the face grabbing, throat filling Conrad. My chest tingles with proud satisfaction that I'm the one who landed these three.

I turn my head to face him, and he spreads my mouth apart with two fingers, salty from his own precome. I swallow down the faint traces of him that he gives me, thirsty for more. With his palm flush to my cheek, he slides his cock between my lips, making my throat spread to accept him. I gurgle and moan, loving the way my pussy pulses in response to being smothered by his hard cock.

Glenn's thighs connect with the undersides of mine as he pushes my legs back, bracing his hands around the backside of my knees. The broad dripping head of him nudges into me, tiny thrust after tiny thrust, giving my pussy time to adjust to each thick inch of him.

Conrad likes feeling his cock in my throat; once his trimmed pubic hair tickles my upper lip and he is all the way in, he slides his thumb along my throat. He groans, discovering the bulge of himself inside me.

Glenn feeds me more cock, sinking into what feels like halfway. I could turn my head to look, but the dark rumbling groans he lets out makes me seize around him, getting more turned on by what feels like the second.

Max leans in, sucking my breast into his mouth as his hips rove forward, still using my hand like his own personal pocket pussy. And I love how solid and slick he is in my palm.

His lips tease out the moment, filling my ear with filthy, unimaginable, exciting things.

"This is right where you belong, Cherry." He traces my lobe with the sizzling tip of his tongue as saliva drips from my spread mouth down my chin and neck. "Taking the Mason men like such a good fucking girl."

I moan at his praise, an undiscovered kink in me coming alive. My walls spasm as Glenn slides deeper inside me for what feels like forever until his groin connects with mine. I feel his day of growth graze my hot, heightened skin before I feel his mouth suck my other nipple deep into his mouth. Rearing his hips back, he slams deep inside me. Pain sears my breast as he sucks me vigorously. Fullness and tearing claw at my lower half until Glenn thrusts into me a few more times. Then the pain takes a backseat to the mind-numbing pleasure.

The generous size of him and the slight swell in his length makes for the ultimate fuck. The cap of him nudges my g-spot, making my insides ache. Conrad hollows my throat, letting me gasp down breaths I didn't even know needed. Smoothing his thumb down the bridge of my nose, he smiles, dark hair mussed and messy. "Good girl," he says before tunneling my throat until I'm flinching back, working desperately to accommodate him and still breathe.

I manage.

Max is still thrusting in my hand when Glenn pulls off my breast, hovering above me on long, ropy arms. "I feel that sweet, tight pussy of yours strangling my cock."

My pussy flutters at his words, and the grin that fans out across his lips steals the breath in my chest. His eyes hold me captive as he says to his sons, "she's ready."

The slap of his body into mine drives me absolutely insane, sending me over the edge in massive crashing waves. I quiver, my cunt squeezes, spasms, my entire core is engulfed in flames. Everything feels so good; Max and Conrad's mouths are on me, I *feel them* everywhere.

"Tell them," Glenn growls through a tight jaw, like he's holding out for as long as he can. He fucks me harder, his long cock spearing through me with delicious force. "Tell them," he commands again, this time holding his weight on one arm to pinch my nipple hard.

"I'm coming," I mumble after Conrad pulls his cock out of my throat long enough for me to speak, surprised to still be drinking his cock down this way. But after I do what Glenn says, I stick out my tongue, coaxing Conrad back to my warm mouth. He slides in and my brain tingles euphorically. Max drives his hips into my fist, feeding me more naughty words.

"Get ready. We're going to fill you full. You'll be leaking Mason men for a week, I promise you, beautiful."

As if it were the cue, Glenn lets loose a wild snarl, beads of his sweat plummeting from his forehead down to my face. Conrad pulls all but the swollen head of his cock out of my mouth, making me focus on just the tip of him as his dad lets loose inside me.

Max jerks his hips back and moves my hand to his balls, not letting me touch his cock.

After popping off Conrad's cockhead, I contemplate protesting at the way the two of them are holding back. But Glenn's voice comes to a halt, his body stilling between my spread thighs. Warmth jets through me in rippling waves, Glenn's eyes squeezed shut as he chants, "Cherry, Cherry, Cherry."

Feeling those balls drain into me makes my clit awaken from her sated state, my nipples perking up, wishing Max and Conrad would pay them attention again.

When I look at my stepbrothers, their eyes are locked on my pussy, transfixed by the come-coated cock sliding in and out of me. The way they so freely love and share me, and are unafraid to take part in each other's pleasure... it makes me insane.

I make a pretty *crazy girl*.

Glenn wrings out the last drops of his heavy sac inside me before sliding out. Wordlessly, Max and Glenn switch positions, and before I can question how the rest of this goes down, my head is back as I moan to the ceiling, Glenn's mouth suckling at my hard nipple.

"That's right, just enjoy. Just enjoy, baby," Conrad coos, dragging the tip of his cock around my jaw, smacking it against my bottom lip.

"Please," I beg him. "Fuck my mouth. *Please.*"

For the first time ever, his pleasing demeanor melts away, leaving behind a dark-eyed, itchy-palmed monster. He lowers his face to mine, the tips of our noses almost kissing. "I'm gonna fill your tight cunt with my seed, Cherry, and only after that can I blow my load down your throat."

"Oh my god!" I moan, and I don't even know if I'm moaning in response to the sinister, sexy as shit side of Conrad I'm just now seeing, or if it's because at that exact moment, Max drives his cock inside me to the hilt.

Maybe it's both. Or maybe it's both and the fact that Glenn is sucking on my tits like he's trying to feed himself.

"Fuck, oh my god," I pant, the entire situation making my entire body begin to tremble. It's like being a kid in a candy store, only you have unlimited money and no parent there to tell you no. I want it all and I want it all now.

And I'm having it.

"I didn't need lube," Max offers, his voice smoky and sexy. He draws out and sinks in slowly. "Dad filled you nice and full. Left you ready." He drives in again, Glenn suckles harder, Conrad slides two fingers onto my tongue, and I begin voraciously sucking off the precome.

Conrad releases me after a moment, and my gaze goes to Max.

"I've waited for this for years, Cherry. Do you know that?" Sweat glistens as it drives down the valley between his pecs, Max completely bare-chested unlike his father. His body is one bred from a god–*obviously*–and trained carefully with discipline. Everything about him is erotic, and I nod, silently begging him to unleash inside of me.

He slides back inside, holding himself so deep that my hole burns as it stretches. Max is thick at the base, long and solid. He hits different spots, and those are spots long ignored. My lower half seizes appreciatively as he says, "I've wanted to fill you full of my come for years." He lowers his lips to mine as Conrad leans back. "*Sis.*"

Rocking back to his knees, Max hammers me hard as my eyes roll back. Conrad squeezes my tit, Glenn's mouth goes to my collarbone, and Max starts to come.

"Fuck," he groans, and his errant curse sends me over. I strain my head off the bed, trying to see where we join as I spasm around him, hard and fast, my pussy pulsing to a different rhythm than with Glenn.

"She's coming," he announces, earning groans from the other two. Conrad's voice is far angrier than Glenn's, and when I finally open my eyes, pussy still seizing, I see him gripping the base of his dick, *hard*.

I milk Max as he fills me, his come flooding my abdomen in shorter but more frequent jets than his dad.

When he pulls out, he and Conrad switch positions, and I can't help but grin. Before positioning himself between my legs, Conrad stuffs a pillow under my tailbone as Max assumes the position at my side, fondling my breast in his large hand. Glenn gets to his knees, holding his cock out. Opening my mouth, he praises me as he slides into my throat. "Good girl cleaning up my cock while you take my son's."

I can't see Conrad, and I can't speak now that I'm sucking the salty sweetness from Glenn's shaft, but I feel his groan vibrate through my body as he sinks inside me. Conrad's cock is thicker than the other two, with almost as much length. The way he moves inside me makes my stomach tingle and my clit throb.

Each of them feels so different, and yet all of them feel so good, I could never choose. I'm glad I don't have to.

"Oh fuck, you're so fucking warm and tight, Cherry," Conrad groans, showing me more and more of his dirty side. My cunt burns as he picks up the pace, and I swallow as Glenn leaks onto my tongue, Max still kneading the peak of my breast with his lips and tongue. He pops off, pinches my nipple and kisses my neck before resuming his latch.

"You have so much Mason come in that sweet cunt of yours. You're ours," Conrad grinds out, shoving inside me for the final time before he too starts spasming.

His unraveling undoes me. I swallow around Glenn, my spine going concave as I push my chest to the ceiling, coming in dramatically long and powerful waves.

"That's right, come with me, drink me down."

Glenn pulls out of my mouth, and I open my eyes, my head volleying around the room to take in the scene. Conrad's release tears through me in rough, fast shots, his head tipped forward to watch himself sink inside of me. Glenn and Max are watching too, and their twisted voyeurism wrings the last of my orgasm from me.

"She's still coming," he announces to them proudly before slowly pulling his softening cock from my cunt.

"You're so full," Conrad says.

"Such a good girl, Cherry," Glenn adds.

Max smiles, hard cock pressed to my thigh as he lathes my

nipple. "You own us now, beautiful. Whatever you want, use us."

"I'm yours," I whisper as my eyes grow heavy and my head falls into the soft down pillow. All the orgasms, all the emotional chasms being filled, all the commotion... I drift off.

I've never slept so well.

Seriously.

And when I wake up, there's a note on the night table that says the shower is ready for me. Padding into the master bath that I've never used, I treat myself to a hot shower, then cocoon myself in plush terry when it's done. After getting dressed, I head down, still feeling groggy and a bit sore. I can't stop lowering my hand between my legs, feeling where they were last night.

It felt so good.

When I make my way into the kitchen, I half expect to find Sylvio washing potatoes or restocking wine. I fully expect that the Mason men have gone to work and left me home to rest and calibrate after yesterday's events.

I'm surprised to find everyone huddled around the vast kitchen island, newspapers, iPads, and coffee cups spread across, my men hovering over them in silent consternation.

Glenn is dressed in joggers and a t-shirt, Max is wearing basketball shorts and a t-shirt, and Conrad is the most formal, in jeans, but donning no shirt or socks. I take them in. All that swoopy, dreamy dark hair, their broad shoulders and knotted cores. I can smell the coffee, but I can smell cologne, bar soap, toothpaste, and warm skin, too. Between my legs stirs with delight. I clear my throat.

Their eyes fall on me with hunger and love, and I realize that as long as I live, I'll never get tired of these eyes on me.

Their appreciation and adoration fuels me, fills me, gives me life. The life I've always wanted.

Every girl wants to feel special. You can be a strong woman and still need to feel special.

"Good morning, beautiful," Glenn says, filling the fourth mug on the counter and walking it to me. He wraps my hands around it, placing a soft kiss on the side of my mouth.

"Morning, Cherry," Max nods, tossing me a short but electrifying wink. He pats his lap. "Come have your coffee over here."

There are extra barstools. Many late-night meetings have happened here with wine and laptops. But I want to sit in his lap. So I do.

Conrad's hand wraps around his brother's neck with a squeeze as he leans down and gives me his version of a good morning kiss, which includes a little tongue and a small moan. I eat it up, adoring the ridge of excitement beneath me coming from Max, the mewls of hunger from Conrad, and the groan of approval that comes from Glenn at witnessing our first morning together.

Our first morning together... in this new life.

Max rubs my thigh as he argues with Conrad, Glenn running interference on their discussion by citing legal briefs and previous cases. Mostly, they go about their conversation and morning, while feeding me morsels of affection throughout.

Glenn said they've all taken the day off because we're taking a day trip. When I ask if I'm invited, Max rolls his eyes. Conrad cups my cheek and runs his thumb over my bottom lip. "You'll never have to ask that again, okay?"

I nod, and Max lowers me to the floor. Glenn refills his mug before turning to me. "We're getting you in some pre-law classes. Law school is three years, you need to finish your undergraduate degree but with an accelerated program and great tutors, you can be done with it all and at our side at the firm in five years."

A lawyer? Me?

"Yes, Cherry, and you will be great." Glenn seems to read my fears.

"If you really didn't want to do this, you wouldn't have to. But you're great at arguing and being defiant, and your memory is solid. Not to mention, you turn men to stone in those pencil skirts," Conrad says, letting his eyes slide down my body to survey my breasts. Breasts that he sucked on just hours ago.

"You're made to be a lawyer," Max adds with a confident nod of his head.

I don't know the first thing about law or even pre-law but I know with the help of my step-dad and step-brothers, it will be okay. The confidence and reassurance they give me makes me feel like anything is possible.

And finally, everything is mine for the taking.

Epilogue

FIVE YEARS LATER

The sun no longer wakes me up. When we first started sleeping in here, the blazing California sun melted through the windows, bleeding across my sleepy eyelids, waking me. As soon as I'd expressed that I'd rather not wake up to the glaring and blinding sun, blackout curtains were installed.

This morning, I'm jostled awake by the weight dipping the end of the bed. Pushing up to one elbow, blinking the dreams away, my eyes settle on the silhouette of a very strong, handsome man with a chest full of peppered hair. He reaches out and squeezes my foot that peeks out from the rumpled mess of blankets and sheets.

"Good morning, my love," Glenn croons, keeping his voice whisper quiet. The way his thumb follows the arch of my foot makes me warm.

"Good morning," I whisper through an inevitable yawn. "Are they okay?"

No longer clean-shaven, Glenn wears a thick beard, the most delectable mixes of blacks and grays. Itching to sift my fingers through it, I raise my hand and wiggle it, earning me a handsome grin.

Carefully, he climbs over me until my hand connects with his face, and I can't help the little groan that comes from deep in my belly at the feel of his stubble grating my skin.

"They're fine. They'll probably be up in another two hours wanting to nurse, though. I gave them the rest of what you pumped yesterday, but," his eyes dance between mine, "they'll want the source when they wake up for the day."

I nod, curling my fingertips into him and pulling my nails down his face.

"They aren't the only ones getting hooked."

His gaze drops to the sheet and bracing his weight on one arm, he hooks a finger on the Egyptian cotton, tugging it down. The graze of thin fabric over my hard, overly sensitive nipples makes me groan a little. Looking down, our gazes idle on my very swollen, full breasts, blue veins at the surface from their sheer density.

He pinches one of my nipples, and white cream bubbles up at the peak, rolling in a heavy drop down the side of my breast.

"They won't be up for two more hours," he repeats the same thing he said a moment ago, yet this time, the message is entirely different.

Rocking back to his knees, he slowly tugs the sheet down, exposing my naked body. The way he takes me in always makes me feel so sexy. How his eyes rove over every inch of me as noises of lust bubble up his throat. I feel like a fucking goddess.

"Then I guess I need some help," I smile, still holding my voice quiet so as not to wake anyone else. He tugs his boxers down, exposing his thick, erect cock, tip glistening.

My legs fall apart for him because ever since that day five years ago, I've never said no to any of them. Not once.

"After this," Glenn says, his mouth discovering the side of my throat as he positions his body over mine, ready to penetrate. "You need to get some more sleep."

"We'll see," I mutter, knowing that after he takes me, there's no way I'll be able to stay awake. But still, even all these years later, I live to light their sparks and make them sizzle... in all ways.

"Not *we'll see*. We need rest for court later, so you *will* go back to sleep until I get the twins up, then you'll go back to bed."

The warm body adjacent to me stirs, and then the one next to it does, too. The room fills with rustled bedding and groans of consciousness as Max and Conrad wake. Max slept by me last night, and Conrad right next to him, with Glenn on my other side.

The bed feels empty without all of us.

"Morning, beautiful," Max yawns, turning on his side to drape a large hand across my flat, bare belly. His touch makes me tingle. Glenn nudges his way inside of me, making my eyes flutter closed.

A moment after he's sunk inside me, the bed dips and Conrad takes the vacant spot next to me.

"Boys, we have a situation," Glenn groans to his sons as he saws in and out of me slowly, warming me up. He always goes slow at first in the mornings, and I let him, never telling him that I'm always ready to take him deep.

Knowing just what to do, I drop my hands to my sides and fill them with hard, hot cock. The three of them always feel so hard, just the touch of turgid flesh makes my pussy clench. But in the morning, after a long night of sleep, they're always *so fucking hard* that my orgasm comes way faster.

Glenn stills, waiting for me to adjust his sons in my palms comfortably, then begins to roll his hips again. A moment later, the unraveling begins as Glenn pumps into me with more force, Max and Conrad each latching onto an overly full, aching breast.

Their first suckles have them guzzling, swallowing in quick rapid-fire bursts until let-down is over. Glenn watches his sons suckle the milk from my full breasts as he fucks me, his eyes full of both pride and jealousy. I reach around the heads buried in my chest and stroke his cheek.

"Leave some for your dad, boys," I say to them while looking at Glenn. He lowers his weight to taste my lips before returning to his knees. Draping my legs over his shoulders, he continues to pound me.

Ever since having babies, I've been insatiable. More than I was before. Things I never thought would make me wet have me dripping. Then again, I don't know if it's as much the *things* as the *men* performing said things.

If you'd have told me five years ago that I'd have my stepbrothers obsessed with my milk, aching and hard in my palms as they nurse on me... I'd have said yeah *fucking* right.

But here I am, my legs trembling under Glenn's grip, sweat dripping down the slope of my arched neck as I writhe, overwhelmed and drunk from all the delight.

I feed my fingers through Max and Conrad's hair, earning me a harder suck from both of them. Warm streams of milk dribble down my breast as Conrad lifts off, finding my eyes.

"I didn't get to tell you good morning," he says as I reward him with a hard pump of his cock. He groans, pressing his lips to mine. He tastes sweet and creamy. "Good morning, baby," he smiles, carving a trail of hot kisses down my chest, back to my leaking breast.

He latches, and continues to drink me down as I pump his cock, Max's too. Glenn's hips roll, and as usual, from watching his sons feed from me, he's close to coming. He's controlling his pumps, not to mention the set of his jaw and the fight in his eyes to not unravel giving him away.

"Rub my clit," I say to him, and I swear before the words leave my mouth his thumb is petting my bundle of nerves, pushing me over the edge.

"There she goes," he groans as my cunt spasms around him, coming in fast, rippling waves. I lift my head, wanting to take in the full sight as I orgasm. The way milk dribbles from Max's pink lips and how his eyes are squeezed tightly shut as if sucking me is the most erotic, intoxicating thing.

Heat spreads through me as Glenn releases himself into me, shot after shot of thick, hot come flooding my insides. His spine straightens while he holds himself deep, coming hard with his eyes on his woman.

Conrad and Max start moving their hips, and I know they're close too. We always all come together, within just a few moments, I swear. Our bodies are in sync that way, and I wouldn't have it any other way.

Conrad gurgles on a mouthful of warm breastmilk, my breast both aching and buzzing from being suckled and made comfortable by a strong, sexy man.

Come rockets up my side, over my breast, and onto my nipple as Conrad orgasms, his head now tipped back in ecstasy, milk lining his upper lip. Max falls over the edge a moment later, his come also ambitiously painting my hip and breast, up to my throat, too.

We lie there, all of us panting and sated, taking in the sight of milk, come, and sweat glistening on me.

At the door comes a tiny knock. One that can only come from the tiniest of fists. Conrad leaps out of bed, jumping into the boxer briefs he discarded last night. "I'll go," he says, rushing to the door.

His voice is a whisper, but still makes me smile when I hear him tell our daughter, "Mama needs some more sleep. You want pancakes? Me and Daddy can make them?"

Our daughter's little voice is still sleepy but determined when she says, "Yes! Yes! Daddy Max makes better pancakes than you though, Daddy."

The bed creaks, Max jumping up as quickly as Conrad did. He dresses, dusting a kiss over my forehead as he makes his way to the door.

"You two rest. We'll get you up in a few hours," he says, beginning to pull the door shut. "If the twins wake up, you want me to bring them in?"

Glenn, still sweaty and panting with my legs draped over him, nods to his son. "Not sure I'm gonna leave them much. Maybe defrost the milk from the weekend. Sylvio put it in the freezer in the pantry."

"Got it." Then the door pulls closed, and I'm left with just Glenn.

I wiggle my eyebrows. "You know, after you get me pregnant again, you'll have to share the morning session with Max and Conrad."

He pulls out of me, his warm come rushing out with his softening cock. With the sheet, he wipes me up between my legs and on my sides, ridding me of Max and Conrad's orgasms.

"I know, but fair's fair," he says, acknowledging the rules we'd set.

When I'm in my three-day ovulation window, only one of them comes inside me. The twins are Max's babies, and our three-year-old daughter is Conrad's. Now it's my stepfather's turn to put another gorgeous dark-haired baby inside of me.

He flops down next to me, his head resting on my arm. His beard grates the sensitive skin of my breast, and when he latches onto my sore nipple and begins to suck, I can't help but moan.

His hand finds my cunt–I'm still sticky from his come and my orgasm. Sliding his fingers up and down my slit, he works on emptying me as I moan at the perfect pressure he's applying.

My hand wraps around him, fishing my fingers into his hair, damp with sweat. He lifts off, pinching my nipple to watch the creamy milk pool at the surface, then his tongue follows the drop down, not letting a molecule go to waste.

"You're so sweet, Cherry. You taste so good."

"Mm," I murmur, nudging him back to my breast.

"We're lucky, you know?" he asks between flicks of his tongue over my hard, sensitive nipple. "Me and my boys."

"Yeah?" I ask, growing heady and detached from the way his thumb strokes down against my swollen clit, from the way his mouth teases my tit.

"Mm," he matches my murmur, sucking my breast into his mouth for another long pull of breastmilk. "We get sweet Cherry Pie *every* fucking day."

I have three wonderful, sweet babies, three perfect handsome men who worship and adore me, and a law degree I'd never have earned if it weren't for their grade-A tutoring and threats of sexual withholding.

Today is my first time in court.

I never knew Satan and his spawn would become and give

me everything, and yet here I am, dozing off, letting that demon seed bake as we work on growing our family.

Someone has to take over Mason Family Law one day.

Afterword

I literally had no idea that I enjoyed reading the nursing kink until a friend recommended a book to me. She mentioned it had the kink and I was interested. It was mild and by the end of the book I realized how much I enjoyed it and wanted more.

I hope you enjoyed it for the over-the-top style. I've always been a fan of the insta/fast-paced in novellas and I thoroughly enjoy writing those big, all encompassing feelings.

If you want more nursing and breeding kink, my new book, book one in the Wrench Kings series, is loaded with it.

If you want to try some of my full-length works and my usual writing style, I recommend starting with book one in the Men of Paradise series, Where Violets Bloom.

Or, I'll Do Anything, which is book one of my Oakcreek series.

Thank you for taking the time to read this novella. I value your time greatly! I hope you enjoyed it and I hope you'll check out my backlist for more contemporary with a twist of taboo type of reads!

AFTERWORD

XO
Daisy

Also by Daisy Jane

Series:

Crave & Cure (3 Books)

Stuck With Tuck / male porn star / MF / Book 1

Cohen's Control / subtle femdom / MF / Book 2

Wrench Kings (3 Books)

The Wild One / a reverse age gap romance / MF / Book 1

The Brazen One / a grumpy/sunshine romance / MF / Book 2

The Only One / a femdom romance / MF / Book 3

Men of Paradise (3 Books)

Where Violets Bloom / a stalker romance / MF / Book 1

Stray / a femdom romance / MF / Book 2

With Force / a CNC romance / MF / Book 3

Oakcreek (2 Books So Far)

I'll Do Anything / a bully femdom romance / MF / Book 1

After the Storm / an alpha MM romance / MM / Book 2

The Millionaire and His Maid (3 Books)

His Young Maid / an age gap boss/employee romance / MF / Book 1

Maid for Marriage / an age gap romance / MF / Book 2

Maid a Mama / a surprise pregnancy romance / MF / Book 3

The Taboo Duet

Unexpected / an age gap Daddy figure romance / Book 1

Consumed / a Daddy kink romance / Book 2

Standalones:

The Other Brother / dual POV / MF

The Corner House / single POV / MFMM, MFM, MFM with an HEA

My Best Friend's Dad / age gap instalove novel / MF

Waiting for Coach / age gap novel / student teacher / MF

Hot Girl Summer / a taboo step sibling romance / MF

Pleasing the Pastor / an age gap virgin romance / MF

Release / a taboo MMF, MM, MF romance

Raleigh Two / a taboo MFM romance / MFM

The Man I Know / a married couple romance / MF

Novellas:

Cherry Pie / very taboo why choose / MFMM

If You Liked This Story...

Leave your review on Amazon! I'd love to hear your feedback.

Thoughtful, comprehensive reviews are the best way to help Indie authors grow, both their skill and their business. Next to reading our books, reviews are the next best gift!

If you have time, I'd love to hear your opinion.

And thank you again for reading!

Sign up for my newsletter to keep up-to-date with my projects, deals on books, sneak peaks, and much more.

About the Author

Daisy Jane is an indie author writing contemporary romance with kink. In her stories you will find small towns, ordinary people and extraordinary sex lives.

When not writing romance, Daisy enjoys reading, finding new ways to eat peanut butter, black coffee, funk music and cool cover bands, Yosemite, browsing Reddit, true crime, and so much more.

She lives in California with her husband of fifteen years, their two daughters and three cats.

facebook.com/DaisyJaneAuthor
twitter.com/authordaisyjane
instagram.com/authordaisyjane

Patreon

I write erotic novellas over on my Patreon. So if you like my writing style but want something shorter in length, I release a chapter every week.

Also, you'll get access to commissioned NSFW art featuring your favorite heroes and heroines from my books, Men of Paradise and Wrench Kings included!

You'll get access to everything in my one and only tier. Quarterly merch coming soon!

Come on, hold my hand.

Patreon.com/DaisyJane

(Content ages 18+)

Printed in Great Britain
by Amazon